I'm smiling because I'm imagining all the ways I'm going to pleasure you.

Destiny gripped the stone in her pocket as panic flooded her chest. It was getting worse. Now she was hearing voices.

There's nothing wrong with you, lovely.

Destiny's gaze caught on the man in the front row. He wore a crisp black suit, black boots and had flung a black raincoat over the seat next to him. His intense green eyes pinned her in place.

She suddenly felt naked as he scrutinized every inch of her fair skin, as if caressing her with his eyes.

No, this couldn't be happening. She couldn't be losing her mind. She squeezed the hematite stone in her palm, hoping to ground herself. Instead, she grew dizzy.

She wouldn't faint, wouldn't lose control of her body....

Dee was strong, she was intelligent, she was... going down.

PAT WHITE

Having grown up in the Midwest, Pat White has been spinning stories in her head ever since she was a little girl—stories filled with mystery, romance and adventure. Years later, while trying to solve the mysteries of raising a family in a house full of men, she started writing romance fiction. After six Golden Heart nominations and a *Romantic Times BOOKreviews* award for Best Contemporary Romance (2004), her passion for storytelling and love of a good romance continues to find a voice in her tales of romantic suspense. Pat now lives in the Pacific Northwest, and she's still trying to solve the mysteries of living in a house full of men—with the added complication of two silly dogs and three spoiled cats. She loves to hear from readers, so please visit her at www.patwhitebooks.com.

SAVING DESTINY

PAT WHITE

Silhouette Books

nocturne™

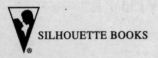

SILHOUETTE BOOKS
®

ISBN-13: 978-0-373-61774-6
ISBN-10:   0-373-61774-7

SAVING DESTINY

Copyright © 2007 by Pat White

This edition published by arrangement with Harlequin Books S.A.

® and TM are trademarks of Harlequin Books S.A., used under license.
Trademarks indicated with ® are registered in the United States Patent
and Trademark Office, the Canadian Trade Marks Office and in other
countries.

www.silhouettenocturne.com

Printed in U.S.A.

Dear Reader,

I've always been fascinated by things we can't see but that we know exist. Love, hope and compassion top the list.

But what about other things, things we may not understand? Other dimensions and other worlds?

I was thrilled when talented authors Michele Hauf, Cynthia Cooke and Nina Bruhns invited me to be a part of the DARK ENCHANTMENTS series. It gave me the chance to dream way outside the box, and research a fascination of mine: crystals. I've always been drawn to their strength and beauty.

I'm also intrigued when people from completely different worlds find common ground and develop understanding and lasting relationships.

So, with a spin of the rose quartz crystal on my desk, I challenge you to leave reality behind and step into the magical world of DARK ENCHANTMENTS.

Cheers,

Pat White
patwhitebooks.com

Saving Destiny is dedicated to the goddess within all of us. Namaste.

Four hundred years ago a secret, hermetic order was created by the first earl of St. Yve and a handful of initiates who pledged their lives to keep the world safe from evil paranormal beings. Ever since, the Cadre has been dedicated to maintaining the delicate balance between the mortal and dark realms through research and observation of otherworldly entities. Seldom does the Cadre interfere.

But not all mortals seek peaceful understanding between the realms. In recent decades, an opposing force has been created by the British Security Service. This covert group, called P-Cell, has but one directive: destroy paranormal creatures of all kinds.

As the two organizations fight faithfully for their separate causes, unbeknownst to either of them the dark forces of evil gather, preparing to overtake the mortal realm....

Prologue

Red-hot flames raced across the city, ravaging buildings, burning the flesh off mortals desperate to escape.

Nero stood on the cliff, watching, a slight curl to his lips. "They will not challenge me again."

"You are pleased," the messenger from the dark realm said. He did not have visible form, not yet.

That would change once the fire burned out, creating precious soft ash, the seed of the future.

Out of the ash a new creation would be born, one of human form, with a demon's soulless heart. The creation would be more intelligent, more sophisticated than any known species of Daemon Sapiens.

"You will be remembered as a great leader," the formless creature soothed.

"Yes, and I will build great palaces. I will call my new city Neropolis."

Of course he would, thought the messenger. The Roman emperor loved himself above all else, and thanks to that love an embryo was being formed from the ashes of the Great Fire of Rome, a sophisticated demon skilled at tempting mortals with their own weakness—their lust for self-importance.

The creature would be called Ash Demon. He would tempt with ego gratification until the mortal felt whole and alive, until the mortal destroyed himself with his own desire to rule as a god.

Fool.

Gods were mere fantasy. In the dark realm, order was maintained by Grigori, the council that conceived of the creation of the sophisticated Ash Demon to help maintain balance.

Balance equaled existence. If the dark and mortal realms lost equilibrium, chaos would ensue and creatures would be sentenced to their own personal hells—for an Ash Demon that meant life as a mortal.

"Our business is done." Nero started down the path toward his burning city.

The messenger of Grigori watched the flames

flicker with joy in anticipation of new creation. Ash Demon would be an intelligent species, cunning and heartless.

Ash warriors would safeguard the passageway used by those of the dark realm to travel back and forth without depending on mortals as their conduit.

Ash Demons would spawn like mortals to sustain their existence. They would rise above the rest with the ability to rule and keep order.

It was Grigori's greatest achievement, made from the ash of mortals.

Chapter 1

Present day
England

"Where is my brother?"

Kadenshar didn't recognize his own weakened voice.

"He's safe," a woman said.

She lied. He felt it in his chest.

"He's dead," he said.

"Not yet."

But soon. Soon the last of his family would be destroyed because of his failure, his weakness.

A cry started deep in his empty soul, burning his chest, rising into his throat. But nothing came out.

He could not see, nor move his mortal limbs.

"What have you done to me?" he rasped.

"We saved you, Kadenshar." A different woman spoke, younger, more innocent than the first. She was mortal and had no right using his given, demon name. He did not have the energy to scold her.

"I can't feel my hands." Had he lost them in the transition from dark realm to mortal world?

"Loosen the bindings," the older female ordered.

Only in the twenty-first century would a woman be in charge of a warrior like Kadenshar.

He heard a crackling sound. Slowly his fingers warmed with feeling as demon blood rushed to his fingertips.

"Why can't I see?"

"We've put a healing cloth on your eyes. You were wounded in battle. Do you remember?"

No. He remembered passing through the traiectus to the mortal world, desperate to stop his younger brother from doing something foolish like getting himself eradicated. Kadenshar's last memory was the sight of Tendaeus through the thick, green forest, conversing with a faerie with bright red hair. An explosion shook the earth, and Kadenshar was knocked to the ground, pounded into the earth by something cold and hard and…

"Where am I?" His voice grew stronger.

"St. Yve Wood. I am Lady Aurora."

He'd heard this name. She was a Cadre leader.

He knew of the Cadre, a group of mortal researchers intent on the study of paranormal entities. Or was their goal domination? Their base was in a castle near the enchanted forest of St. Yve Wood where otherworldly entities and mortals coexisted. Some paras thought it a safe place; others considered it a demon's torture cell.

"You came to make war," Lady Aurora said. "P-Cell agents shot you and your warriors."

P-Cell, of course—the mortal death merchants created by British Intelligence to destroy any and all paras, including Ash Demons like Kadenshar.

"I came for my brother," he said. "Alone." He did not cross over with soldiers intent on war.

"Your brother crossed over looking for battle."

"He was wounded?"

"Yes. We're holding him in a crystal to stop the degeneration process," Lady Aurora said.

"Why?"

"He was wounded by heavy artillery. He's sustained serious injuries to his human form."

"No, why did you bring us here?"

"We saved you," the younger female said.

Saved? At the mercy of mortals only once before, Kadenshar knew they were selfish beings intent on self-gratification. If they were helping him, they had a secondary motive.

"What do you want from me?"

Low whispers echoed in the chamber. Cold.

Dark. He couldn't see with his mortal eyes, but his Ash Demon sense told him he was being held deep in the earth.

Imprisoned. By mortals.

Worse than eradication.

"We want you to bring us Destiny, the great crystal healer," Lady Aurora said.

"The creature that threatens our existence?"

"That is folklore, not fact."

Kadenshar fisted his hands. He'd heard the stories of a girl, part human, part angel, who would grow up to become a Crystal Goddess, a healer and peace-maker.

A goddess that would have the power to end the existence of the Ash Demon race.

His race, his people that he had sworn to protect upon his father's death.

"If you want your brother to live, you will help us," Lady Aurora said. "You will find Destiny and bring her to St. Yve."

"I will kill her first."

"No, you won't. She can help your brother. She has the power to heal his wounds. If you bring her to us, we will release your brother and you will both be allowed to return to your world."

"That she, in turn, will destroy."

"That is not true."

"How do you know this?"

She did not answer.

"She will turn thirty soon," Lady Aurora continued. "You need to find her before her birthday."

"Why have you chosen me?"

"We know your family's history. You are intelligent leaders."

If she knew their history, she also knew their weakness: Kadenshar's illness that had caused his father and his older brother to seek mortal help. They were killed for their efforts.

It was his fault. It would always be his fault.

"You are a great warrior, Kadenshar. You are the only one who can protect her and bring her here. She won't come willingly. She fears and denies her gifts."

Her gifts should be the least of her worries. He'd heard that a plan was under way by fellow Ash Demons to destroy the would-be goddess. They couldn't kill her or they'd risk destroying the traiectus, their passageway to the mortal realm. Instead their plan was to attack her mind, twist her thoughts until she went mad.

As a mere mortal she would have little defense against the spells. But as a Crystal Goddess she would be able to fight back.

Kadenshar wanted to fight right now. He wanted to rip off his bindings, find his brother and leave this tomb.

"P-Cell agents nearly killed you," Lady Aurora said. "I saved you because I need your help. Destiny can bridge the gap between the mortal and dark realms. It's the best chance for peace."

And it would save his brother's life.

"Please consider our offer," she said. "We'll leave you to rest."

He heard footsteps, a door close and a dead bolt slide into place. His wrists were still bound to his sides, his eyes still covered.

Kadenshar had long given up on peace but not on duty, duty to his only remaining sibling. Theirs was a strained relationship. Tendaeus had never recovered from his eldest brother and beloved father dying while on a mission to help the youngest child, Kadenshar.

Only later did they discover that Kadenshar would outgrow the Ash Demon illness, that his father and brother's lives had been lost in vain.

His mother was relieved that Kadenshar would live, yet she never looked at him with the same appreciation in her eyes.

Of course not. He'd caused the deaths of half of his family. Kadenshar struggled with the shame every moment of his existence. For Tendaeus, rage buried itself deep. Tendaeus had decided that exacting revenge by killing mortals would bring him peace for his family's tragedy. Instead it had imprisoned them both: Tendaeus in a crystal at the mercy of his captors; Kadenshar stripped of free will, ordered to protect and save a creature that could destroy his very existence.

Then again, if he possessed Destiny he would have the power to save his brother and his people.

He must possess her, control her mind, her body

and desires. Using the Ash Demon gift, he would expose her ego, seduce her with her need for warped self-grandiosity—the human flaw that had created the sophisticated Ash Demon race out of fire. He would break her down until she was totally dependent on him, needing him in a way she'd needed no other man.

She wouldn't realize she'd been lured by a demon until it was over. He'd persuade her to release his brother, and Kadenshar and Tendaeus would return to their world, away from the filth of mortals and their petty needs. They would be gone by the time Destiny realized she'd fallen in love with the very creature she'd been put on this earth to destroy.

She would have fallen deeply in love and would be destroyed from the inside out, having lost faith in everything.

Especially herself.

Destiny Rue struggled against growing panic when she spotted her mother in the front row.

Her dead mother.

Breathe. That's it. Slowly. In through the nose, exhale through the mouth. Count to five. One. Two. Three. Four—

"Dr. Rue?" Dean Sodenheim prompted.

Dee gripped the wooden podium and glanced at the audience filling the small theatre at Seattle University.

The image of her dead mother had vanished. Thank God.

The spells were getting worse and more frequent.

No, she wouldn't accept that. Dee was suffering from low blood sugar aggravated by stress. After all, she wasn't scheduled to make the presentation today and was terrified of public speaking.

"Dr. Walingford hopes to join us shortly," she started. "Until he arrives I will begin the presentation on the Natural Resource Seven study, considered a groundbreaking treatment for migraine headaches."

Groundbreaking? Hardly. NR7 was another one of Walingford's manipulations, a way to keep the grant money flowing while enjoying his four-day workweeks and long lunches.

Sliding her hand into her lab coat pocket, she brushed her thumb against the cool gray stone. It had always calmed her, ever since she was a little girl. It was one of the many stones from her mother's collection.

Stones that were Dee's only link to her estranged and insane mother.

Dee nodded at Professor Sodenheim and he dimmed the lights. Good. The students, professors and other guests wouldn't see her trembling fingers as she worked the remote control. She felt safer in the dark, more relaxed.

She started the presentation and images flashed on the screen. "Our laboratory has held clinical trials of seven elements that, in combination, would

reduce stress and strengthen the human body's ability to fight infection, both of which could trigger
migraine headaches."

Strengthen the human body? What a joke. The
body was weak, flawed and prone to idiosyncrasies
that rendered it helpless.

Walingford had given her a script to read from,
not wanting her to go off course and share information beyond her scope of expertise.

Jerk. To think he'd lured her to Quar Labs with
compliments on her thesis, telling her she was
exactly the kind of scientist he needed on his team.
She'd believed his false sincerity, signed a two-year
contract and discovered that, instead of pursuing
her innovative theories about a new drug combination to treat mental illness, Walingford wanted her
to focus on the study of natural remedies.

Sure, that's what everyone was into these days:
healing thyself using mind over matter.

Ridiculous. The brain was the most flawed organ
of all. Look at how it tricked her today, flashing the
image of her crazy, dead mother in the front row.

"Some patients exhibited immediate relief two to
four hours after treatment," she started, "while
others took up to eight hours to respond. The first
element is a cool, peaceful environment."

To fully engage the audience, she should make
eye contact now and then. She mustered her
strength, hoping she wouldn't see dear ole Mom
smiling back at her.

"We've concluded that a peaceful, safe environment sets the foundation for the healing process."

She held her breath and glanced up. No Mom. She sighed with relief.

Some students studied the screen intently while others gazed off into space.

Then her gaze caught on a strange-looking man in the front row. He looked…exotic, with long, dark hair pulled loosely back. He wore a crisp black suit and black boots, and had flung a black raincoat over the seat next to him. His intense green eyes pinned her in place. How could she know the color from this far away?

A slight smile curved his lips. Was he laughing at her?

I'm smiling because I'm imagining all the ways I'm going to pleasure you.

She gripped the stone in her pocket as panic flooded her chest. It was getting worse. Now she was hearing voices.

"Step two is the temperature," she continued, changing the slide. She'd have to see her neurologist.

There's nothing wrong with you, lovely.

"Maintaining a cool environment, about sixty degrees, is considered crucial for the process to be effective," she said on autopilot.

The stranger's smile faded, but his gaze didn't waver. Suddenly she felt naked as he scrutinized every inch of her fair skin as if caressing her with his eyes.

Heat rushed to her cheeks. She snapped her attention to her notes.

"Step three is sound," she croaked. She pressed the remote for the next screen.

The soothing sound of rain echoed in the theater. She glanced at the screen, and a gasp caught in her throat at the sight of a man and a woman having sex. She snapped her attention to the audience. No one seemed to notice.

No, this can't be happening. I can't be losing my mind.

She was tired, overworked and stressed out and she hadn't eaten since lunch…yesterday. She needed something to stabilize her blood sugar and quick.

I've got something for you…

She coughed, and Professor Sodenheim motioned to the glass of water on the podium. She nodded, sipped and continued to read from her script.

She couldn't look at the screen, couldn't look at the sexy man in the audience. Staring at her notes, she said, "Step four is touch."

I will touch you, my sweet. Tracing my warm fingers down the valley between your breasts, to your rib cage, past your belly button…

She squeezed the hematite stone in her palm, hoping to ground herself. Instead she grew dizzy.

She wouldn't faint, wouldn't lose control of her body…her mind, like her mother.

Dee was strong, she was intelligent, she was…
Going down.

Dee opened her eyes and struggled to focus.

Vibrant green eyes, the color of the forest after a long, saturating rain, smiled back at her.

The stranger's eyes.

"How are you feeling?" he asked, his voice brushing against her skin like a calm breeze on a fall afternoon.

She didn't answer at first, struggling to fight off her disorientation. Where was she again? What had happened?

"You fainted during your presentation," he said as if reading her thoughts.

"I fainted," she repeated.

"Yes."

"I've got candy." Sonya, Dee's work partner, came into focus next to the stranger. "You scared the hell out of us. You have to remember to eat, girl."

"Okay," was all Dee could say.

Sonya shouldered the man out of the way. He stood and glared at her back. Dee hoped he never looked at *her* that way.

"Good thing Walingford showed up when he did," Sonya said.

"The presentation…" Dee struggled to sit up.

Sonya placed her hand on Dee's shoulder. "It's fine. Walingford is finishing up. Should I call the paramedics?" Sonya glanced at the green-eyed man. "She has hypoglycemia."

"I'll be fine," Dee assured.

The green-eyed man stepped into the shadows of the room. She wondered who he was and why he was so interested in her.

Walingford burst into the room. "She's awake?"

"Yes," Sonya answered.

He towered over Dee. "And you look fine. Good. I won't feel guilty about firing you."

Sonya shook her head as if advising Dee to keep quiet. Walingford had his moments, his fits of anger that he conveniently forgot the next day. Sometimes Dee wondered if he was bipolar.

"Now, Karl," Dean Sodenheim said, walking in behind him. "That's being a little harsh. The girl is sick."

"The girl is a weak link on my team if she can't handle a simple lecture. I will terminate her contract and she can find a less stressful position."

The pompous jerk was researching humane ways to treat migraines yet didn't have a humane bone in his body.

"Unfortunate," the green-eyed man said from the corner of the room.

Dean Sodenheim turned. "Mr. Sharpe, I didn't realize you were here. Dr. Walingford, let me introduce you to Mr. Kade Sharpe, a representative from the ADL Trust. They are interested in broadening their funding of medical research."

Dee sighed. Could this get any worse? She'd blown it big-time in front of a potential financial backer.

The men shook hands. Distaste colored Mr. Sharpe's expression as he retrieved his hand from Walingford's. She'd laugh if she weren't stressed about being suddenly unemployed.

"I'm sorry to hear you plan to fire Dr. Rue," Mr. Sharpe said. "Her doctoral thesis is what prompted us to consider your program."

"Yes, we found her theories intriguing as well, but proved them ineffective and decided to focus on NR7 instead."

Liar. Walingford never tested her hypotheses about the synthetic drug combination that would neutralize brain transmitters. He'd signed her on, locked her in his lab and put her to work. She'd often wondered if he'd hired her to control his competition.

"Come to my office and we'll talk more about NR7." Walingford motioned to Mr. Sharpe.

"I'd rather not."

"Mr. Sharpe?" Dean Sodenheim questioned.

"Dr. Rue's theories intrigue us at ADL. I'd like her to accompany me back to our headquarters in London." He eyed Walingford, who seemed to fidget under Mr. Sharpe's scrutiny. "A good-faith gesture. You release her to us in London for two weeks, and ADL will offer a grant of no less than five hundred thousand dollars for continued field studies supporting NR7."

Wow, she was worth half a million dollars?

Walingford stuck out his hand. "Fine. Dr. Rue will accompany you to London as soon as she's able." He shot her an arrogant smirk, quite pleased with himself that he'd gotten rid of her and made money off the deal.

Anger throbbed in her already aching head. Neither of them consulted her.

"That might be a problem," she said, sitting up. She fought off light-headedness. "You fired me, remember?"

"I withdraw my termination of your contract— which, by the way, has four months left on it. You'll spend as much time as necessary with Mr. Sharpe and the executives at ADL."

She felt like a piece of used lab equipment being sold at auction.

"And if I don't want to go?"

"Dee, it's London," Sonya said.

Destiny didn't care. These men where shuffling her around like a pea in a shell game. She couldn't stand being out of control, pushed around and manipulated. Next they'd be telling her what to eat and when.

Then again, if she'd eaten on schedule she wouldn't have fainted in the first place.

"I won't force Dr. Rue to do anything she's not comfortable with."

Good. Mr. Sharpe respected her.

Then a mischievous smile curved the corner of

his lips. "But I would like to discuss the proposition." He glanced at Walingford. "Alone."

Walingford's lips pinched into a thin line. "Of course."

"Do you want me to stay?" Sonya offered.

"No, I'll be fine."

They left Dee alone with this odd, magnetic man. She studied him, wondering what it was about him that intrigued her so.

Mr. Sharpe leaned against the wall and crossed his arms over his chest. Up close, she could tell his pants were a high-quality, expensive wool, and his shirt was a soft material with a slight sheen that made her want to reach out and brush her fingertips across it.

"You have a brilliant mind," he started.

Right, a mind that was a ticking bomb. After today's episode, could she keep blaming her spells on low blood sugar?

"My associates have asked that I make you a private offer. Accompany me to London where you'll be given everything you need to pursue your own program."

"My own program?"

"Synthetics to numb the neurotransmitters, for instance? If that's how you want to treat migraine headaches then that is what you will study. This has nothing to do with Professor Walingford's program."

"But you're giving him a grant."

"To get possession of you."

"Excuse me?" *Possession?* Like a piece of property?

"That sounded odd. I apologize. I'm struggling with jet lag." He glanced at his expensive black boots. A few seconds passed.

He looked truly apologetic. Which made him that much sexier.

"ADL executives would like your help." He looked up. She'd never seen a shade of green like that before. "You'll direct your own research team. No contract, no long-term commitments for as long as it suits you. Our council thinks it can learn from you."

"I'm a twenty-nine-year-old researcher who just passed out in front of a hundred people."

"Because you put your work before your health. You're dedicated." Pushing away from the wall, he paced to the office window. "I'm equally as determined." He glanced over his shoulder and winked. "To keep *my* job."

"I should be, too, I guess."

"This is the best of all worlds, Dr. Rue." He turned to her. "Your boss will be pleased, you will keep your job and you will lead your own studies in Europe. How can you reject my offer?"

Not easily. Not at all. What was holding her back?

"I can tell you're unsure," he said. "How about I pick you up tonight at seven o'clock? We'll discuss it over an extravagant meal of roasted lobster tail. Or filet mignon if you'd prefer. We'll drink expensive champagne, discuss your trepidation...and by the end of the evening I will convince you to fly with me to London. However, if for any reason you are still uneasy, I will respect your decision to decline my offer."

How could she say no to expensive champagne and a hearty dinner as opposed to her usual yogurt cup with granola? Maybe she'd even order crème brûlée for dessert. Her mouth started to water.

"You really know how to tempt a girl."

"So I've been told."

Chapter 2

He hadn't expected it to be so easy.

Kadenshar relaxed at an espresso shop down the street from Destiny Rue's apartment building. He entertained himself by watching mortals wander in and out, so consumed with their pitiful, narrow lives they couldn't sense bigger forces at work. Dark forces.

He leaned back in his chair, taking a deep breath, struggling to feel centered and grounded in his mortal skin. Although he'd made dozens of visits to the mortal realm when necessary, he had yet to feel comfortable in his human body. An intense vibration floated beneath the surface of his skin, making him uneasy, uncomfortable.

Guilt settled low. *Uncomfortable* didn't begin to describe his brother's fate, locked away in the crystal torture chamber.

Although the Cadre claimed to use crystal storage as a humane alternative to destruction, Kadenshar had heard stories from Ash Demons that survived time spent in the crystal prisons—stories of torture, stories of demons begging for eradication. He'd heard it described as a million jagged knives pricking their mortal skin or claws ripping them open and tearing out that human organ that kept mortals alive, the beating heart. There were other stories…

He shuddered and sipped his extra hot espresso.

They needed to get back to England as soon as possible, yet pressuring her would only cause suspicion, and it was going so smoothly.

A rush of heat crept up his spine. A demon was close.

"Behind you," a man said.

Kade turned to see Ash Demon Pagroe standing over him.

"You should not sneak up on friends like that," Kade said, shaking his hand as mortals did in greeting.

Pagroe joined him at the small table. "Friends? An interesting concept."

The truth was, Pagroe and Kadenshar shared a strained, adversarial acquaintance. He sensed Pagroe had been jealous of Kade's natural leadership abilities and the Grigori's preference of Kadenshar as warrior leader.

"I'm sorry to hear about your brother," Pagroe said.

Was he sympathizing or driving the knife in deeper? Kade wasn't sure.

"I have not given up," Kade said. "I will free him from the crystal prison."

"And how will you do that?"

"Trickery," he evaded.

"You've made some kind of deal with the Cadre?" Pagroe's expression brightened.

He probably hoped Kadenshar would be betrayed by the mortal group of researchers.

"I will do what is necessary to free my brother," Kade said, not using Tendaeus's name in public.

Ash Demons were careful not to draw unwanted attention to themselves. Using their demon names around mortals would definitely spark interest since they were unusual names derived from Roman ancestors.

He stood and motioned for Pagroe to join him at a corner table where they wouldn't be overheard.

"As long as your plan doesn't involve letting the healer get close to the traiectus," Pagroe warned, taking a seat across from Kadenshar. "She could destroy our ability to travel to the mortal world."

"I wonder about the truth to these stories," he said, trying to downplay the importance of the girl. Kade needed her for his own purpose. He didn't want to encourage Pagroe's interest.

"Legends and prophecies have been around long before our time," Pagroe offered. "Like the one about the great Crystal Goddess and the Warrior Demon joining forces. Do you believe that one?"

This question was a test.

"Absolutely not," Kadenshar said. "That is rumor originated by the Cadre. Wishful thinking on their part because they claim to want peace between our worlds."

"And the prophecy about the Crystal Goddess destroying Ash Demons?"

Kade leaned forward. "She is but a weak mortal, easy for an Ash Demon warrior like myself to control."

"Be careful of your arrogance," Pagroe warned.

"You mean my confidence?"

"Don't be too confident, my friend. I wouldn't want you to be lost to us. You have diplomacy skills like no other."

Now he was complimenting Kade? What was this demon up to?

"Not to worry." Kade sipped his espresso.

"I won't. I have a plan, as well, to neutralize the threat."

"Don't get in my way, friend. I must do this not only for my brother but for my family's honor."

"I understand. Just know I will be ready if you fail."

He sounded too hopeful.

"In order for my strategy to work, I need to build

her trust and confidence," Kade said. "I can't do that if you are orchestrating a campaign to drive her insane."

Pagroe leaned back and laughed out loud. "You suspected my hand behind the slide show at the university?"

"A fornicating couple? Who else would it be?"

"I do have fornication on my mind most days. It's a condition from being in this mortal state." He leaned forward, his expression suddenly serious. "Do you know the prophecy, the one about making love to the healer?"

"I know it."

"When does she turn thirty?"

"In a few weeks."

"Excellent. You'll have her in your bed before her birthday and strip her of her powers."

"Ah, but she would have to fall in love in order for that to happen."

"Good point. An impossibility," he teased.

"Then again, after she turns thirty, I could mate with her and assume her powers long enough to free my brother and the others in the crystal chamber."

"And if she destroys you in the process?"

"A female mortal? Not possible. I will focus on freeing my brother, which will give me strength."

"There are—" Pagroe hesitated "—other Ash who think you are selfish, that if it comes to saving Ash Demons or your brother, you will betray us for your own."

"Everything I've done, I've done for the future of our kind. That is why the Grigori named me leader."

"Your father was leader once, before he…" His voice trailed off as he fingered his espresso cup.

"Before what?"

Pagroe cocked his head to the side. "Your father betrayed the Ash to save you."

Kadenshar's temper burned white-hot in his chest. "It wasn't just me. He went in search of a cure for a disease that has destroyed many young Ash."

"But not you."

No, not Kadenshar. Although he'd suffered from the mental torture of the Ash disease that left him in a coma-like state, he'd outgrown the condition within months after his father's death.

Guilt ravaged Kadenshar's mind when he thought about how his father and older brother had died trying to save him. He had never forgiven himself for their deaths.

"The Grigori has faith in you," Pagroe said. "But others do not know you as well as I do. There is a campaign to destroy the healer. They will not listen to anyone—not the Grigori, not you."

"If they kill her, the traiectus will be closed infinitely, preventing us from moving from the dark to the mortal realm at will. Wherever an Ash rests at that moment is where he will exist forever. An Ash will die if stuck in the mortal world and will die if not able to taste it from time to time."

"They won't kill the healer," Pagroe explained.

"They will destroy her rational thoughts. Her thoughts and healing powers are dangerous."

"She is not strong enough to be a threat."

"Some disagree."

"Not only do I have to fight the Cadre to free my brother but I must fight my own kind as well?"

This was growing more complicated. And Kadenshar did not want complicated, he wanted simple.

Lure her. Simple. Seduce her. Simple. Control her. Simple.

Save his brother.

Save his people.

Simple.

"I have upset you," Pagroe said, feigning remorse.

"I am not upset." He sat back and eyed his companion. "I am frustrated that my plan might be disrupted by Ash, by their fear. I am disappointed they have such little faith in me."

"You are a quiet leader, Kadenshar. They can't tell what you are thinking."

"They know my family is one of honor and integrity. That should be enough."

Honor and integrity, the two reasons the Cadre chose him to bring Destiny back to England. How ironic. The very traits they were counting on were the ones he would use to save his brother and maintain control over Ash Demon existence.

Mortals be damned.

They were self-absorbed, horrible creatures. His father had sought out a mortal for the elixir to save Kadenshar. Instead of giving him the means to save his son, the female mortal had set a trap. Kade's father and brother had died at the hands of brutal P-Cell agents, mortal warriors sworn to eradicate any and all paras.

"I will not interfere," Pagroe said. "But the Grigori has requested I stay close."

"To spy on me?" Kadenshar said with humor in his voice. He did not want Pagroe to think Kadenshar considered him a threat, although he didn't trust the demon.

"They requested I keep watch and report on your progress," Pagroe said.

"I would never betray the Grigori. My father did not betray them."

"He exposed the traiectus when he went in search of a cure for your disease."

"He could not have known the female would betray him."

"He should not have trusted a female mortal. Yet he chose to cross over, putting all of us at risk."

Kadenshar wanted to defend Father but couldn't, not without revealing what he feared deep in his heart: that a strong mortal element hummed in his family's seed, and they could be seduced by emotions such as compassion and...love.

The dreaded emotion that made an Ash no better than a mortal.

"Kade?"

He glanced at Pagroe, who wore a quizzical expression. Kade could not allow his adversary to sense his fears.

"Don't worry." Kade smiled. "I will fulfill my duty."

Pagroe stood and bowed. *"Caveo."*

"I will, thank you."

Dee rifled through her closet looking for something appropriate to wear for dinner. Her usual uniform of black slacks, a loose blouse and serviceable low-heeled pumps wouldn't do. Okay, so she wasn't fashionable or trendy.

Yet she suspected her date would look as if he'd stepped off a photo shoot for *GQ* magazine. Or *Spin* magazine? Mr. Sharpe puzzled her, a combination of sophisticated class and wild punk rocker with his long, dark hair and black outfit. He looked mysterious and powerful…and sexy.

"You really are losin' it."

Which reminded her: she should call her doctor and see about medication before she left town—medication for her hypoglycemia, not her inherited craziness.

"I will not accept that, especially not now." No, she couldn't lose her mind just as she was about to make a real contribution to society with her research. There was nothing wrong with her mentally. It was a physical challenge—low blood sugar—that caused her hallucinations. Just thinking the H word shot panic through her stomach.

"Nope, not going there," she said.

She eyed an old bridesmaid's dress. It was a satin low-cut style with beads around the neckline and a bow trimming the back. The color could only be called *electric-lime*.

"Too cheesy," she whispered. "I have to have a simple black thing in here somewhere."

She'd worn it for her sister's engagement party. Dee had been shocked that big sister Annalise had even invited her. Being ten years apart, Dee had felt like an only child growing up with a strange creature called a teenager living in the attic.

And a mother on permanent leave of absence.

"Ah, why am I thinking about you so much, Mom?" she whispered, then realized the reason: Dee's birthday was three weeks away. Another birthday would pass without a homemade birthday cake, girlie presents or a special girls' day out courtesy of a loving mother.

Truth was, her sister and her father wouldn't make much of Dee's birthday, and they were very much alive. They had no use for the baby of the family. The "crazy baby," as Aunt Kay used to call her.

In any other family, the term *crazy baby* would be cute, but not in the Rue family. Crazy was something you feared with ever fiber of your being.

Dee had always sensed that Dad blamed her for

her mother's condition. Postpartum depression after having Dee had affected the chemicals in Mom's brain and she'd never fully recovered. The chemical imbalance developed into insanity, and insanity drove Mom out of the mental hospital and into the street where she was hit by a car and killed on impact.

"You really are morbid."

Darn it, she shouldn't be morbid, not today. She was about to embark on an adventure in Europe, finally being rewarded for her studies and hard work.

Her mother's issues were not her own. Dr. Keen had said she suffered from low blood sugar, that's all. She believed the doctor; she believed in medical science. Maybe if Dad would have believed more in the doctors he would have forced Mom to take the meds keeping her stable, at home and…alive.

A sudden knock made her jump. Great—pensive *and* anxious. Not a good combination when you wanted to make an impression on a man.

She looked through the peephole and spied her neighbor, Adam, pacing the hallway. She opened the door. "Hey, what are you doing here?"

"I heard about you passing out at work. Sonya called." He strode into her apartment. "How do you feel? Did you call the doctor? What can I do to help?"

"Uh, let's see…fine, no and not unless you've got a sexy black dress, size eight, you can lend me."

He froze, turned and stared her down. "Did you say 'sexy'?"

She and Adam had tried the dating thing, but it fizzled before it lit. They were too different: Adam was about experiencing the world by jumping from airplanes, and Dee was about controlling her world with twenty strokes of the toothbrush and thirty-minute power walks. Theirs had grown into a brother-sister relationship, which she appreciated. Only, sometimes Adam seemed a bit overly protective.

"I didn't mean sexy," she said. Or did she? "I meant stylish. You know, sophisticated."

"You mean you don't want to look like your usual scientist-in-lab-coat self?"

"Correct."

"Why?"

She ambled to her front closet and rifled through the clothes. "Didn't Sonya tell you that, too?"

"She did not." He sat on her couch and eyed a copy of *American Scientist* magazine.

"I have a date tonight," she announced.

He put down the magazine and stared her down. "A date?"

"A man from the ADL Trust has made me an offer to accompany him to Europe. ADL is affiliated with London University and they're interested in my graduate studies research, not what I've been working on for Walingford."

"What kind of offer?"

"Total freedom researching my combination of

drugs to treat mental illness. I can take my time. In London. Can you believe it?"

"Sounds too good to be true."

"Cynic."

"I'm a realist. What's his name? Did you see his ID? Why did he show up now?"

"Why not?"

"I don't like it."

"You're being awfully suspicious considering your trust-the-universe nature."

"I don't trust the universe when it comes to you, Dee. You're too gullible."

She turned back to the closet. "Gee, thanks."

"I'm sorry, I didn't mean to hurt your feelings." He went to her and put his arm around her shoulders, eyeing her pathetic wardrobe.

The strange thing was, she felt no warmth, either sexual or platonic, from Adam. She couldn't remember the last time she'd felt a true connection to another living soul.

She broke the connection and went into the galley kitchen. "How about tea?"

"Sure." He positioned himself back on the couch.

She put on the kettle, fighting back the melancholy growing in her chest. She considered herself an excellent scientist, detail-oriented and determined. Yet emotionally she'd been damaged from the lack of a mother's love.

Dee had learned to detach from people, not ask for anything or expect anything.

To be satisfied being alone.

Only, some days the ache in her chest was overwhelming with the thought of what she would never have.

Is that why she was so agreeable about flying to London with a stranger? Because she was desperate to be wanted by someone?

Anyone?

"I think you should check this guy out before you fly away with him," Adam offered.

"You're probably right."

"I always am." He shot her a smile over his shoulder.

Now there was a man who cared about her. Why couldn't she feel anything for him?

Mr. Sharpe picked her up promptly at seven in a limousine. If he wanted to impress Dee, it was working. He'd changed into an expensive black suit accented with a deep red vest.

On anyone else it might have looked gaudy. On Mr. Sharpe it looked scrumptious.

Oh, Lord, had she really thought *scrumptious?*

"I hear the food at Salty's is delicious," he said.

She snapped her attention away from the window and eyed him. "Yes, I've heard that, too," she croaked, embarrassed that while he'd been thinking of their meal, she'd been thinking about him.

"You're troubled by something? What is it?" he asked.

"I'm still trying to process everything that has happened today."

"Don't hurt yourself," he teased. "It's simple. Tonight I'll convince you to accompany me to London and continue your research. You will fulfill your destiny."

An odd expression.

"Tell me more about the department that's funding this project," she asked.

"At dinner," he said. "We have all night."

A sudden flash of herself, naked, at the hands of Mr. Sharpe, made her skin tingle. She plastered a smile on her face and glanced back out the window as they crossed the West Seattle Bridge. Was he flirting with her? She wouldn't know. Dee hadn't properly flirted since…since forever.

Truth was, romance and relationships were not on her priority list. Or, more likely, she wasn't the alluring type.

The exact opposite of her mother.

She'd seen pictures of her mom pre-insanity. Adrianna Rue had been striking, with creamy fair skin, red hair and big green eyes, none of which were gifted to Dee.

No, Dee had an ordinary oval-shaped face with gray-blue eyes and boring lips. She didn't stand out in a crowd. Heck, she'd barely be noticed if she stood naked in the middle of Pike Place Market.

He smiled at her. "You look lovely this evening. Quite enchanting."

She wondered if he had some kind of mind-reading skills. He seemed to sense the direction of her treacherous thoughts.

"You should be honored that the department is offering this opportunity, Destiny. They wouldn't offer it to just anyone."

"How did you become involved with the department?" she asked.

"They recruited me."

"From?"

She noticed a twitch in his jaw as he glanced out his window. Avoiding her question? Interesting.

"From my previous position." He pinned her with his cool green eyes. "I'm an independent contractor."

"You live in London, then?"

"You ask many questions."

"Sorry, just trying to make conversation."

"You don't have to make conversation to fill silence. There's nothing to be nervous about."

He smiled and her heart warmed.

"That is a beautiful necklace," he said.

"Thank you."

"But not nearly as beautiful as the woman wearing it," he whispered.

He reached out to touch her hand, which rested on her thigh.

Images flashed across her mind: lying naked on a bed of gold satin sheets, Mr. Sharpe climbing on top of her, leaning forward to kiss her, his mouth warm and gentle, moving lower, to her neck, then her breast, laving the nipple, the peak hardening with need.

But their connection wasn't solely about sex. It was about completeness and serenity. As his need pressed between her legs, she opened to him, wanting to join their bodies, their souls—

Her head snapped back, bursting the images into pieces.

"Sorry about that," the driver apologized.

They were stopped in front of the restaurant. What had just happened?

Her door opened and Mr. Sharpe offered her his hand.

She stared at the solid, masculine fingers, wondering why his touch had set off such erotic images. It wasn't simple lust that filled her mind, it was more.

It felt real.

She smiled, touched him briefly and snatched her hand away once she had sure footing on the asphalt parking lot.

"You look pale," he said.

"I haven't eaten much today." She didn't look at him. She couldn't. Would he sense her delusion?

Oh, God, she couldn't keep denying the possibility that she had inherited the family insanity. Maybe she hadn't eaten much today, but she ate a piece of cheese and an apple after she'd left work. That should have been enough to stabilize her blood sugar.

How could she keep blaming her spells on hypoglycemia? She was a scientist, for mercy's sake. The data was all too obvious: the dreaded age was creeping up on her. The same age her mom went nuts.

He cupped her elbow and guided her up the stairs.

"What is it?" he asked. "Something is troubling you."

"Nothing." She forced a smile. "It's been a rough week."

A rough year. A rough life.

No, she would not feel sorry for herself. She must achieve her dream as a scientist and make a difference, even if she had to hide a medical condition to do it.

At least if she could get to London and start the project she could train others to carry on without her. Then she might be remembered as a scientist, not the crazy daughter of a lunatic mother.

"You're too hard on yourself." He opened the restaurant door for her.

God, if he only knew how perfect his responses were to her mental thrashing right now.

"You should appreciate your gifts and not worry about what others think."

He gave the hostess his name and she led them to a table overlooking Puget Sound. Across the Sound, the city of Seattle sparkled with night lights. Once seated, she took a slow, deep breath and studied the menu.

"That is what's happening, isn't it?" he said.

"I'm sorry?" She glanced at him. Genuine concern shadowed his soft green eyes.

"You're worried about your boss, your friends at work and what they'll think? Or is it your mother?"

She pinched the menu between her fingers. "My mother?"

The waitress approached their table. "May I start you with something to drink this evening?"

"Champagne," Mr. Sharpe said, then looked at Destiny for her approval.

"That's fine."

He pointed to his selection on the menu. The waitress nodded and left.

"What did you mean, 'your mother'?" she asked.

"Most women are worried about pleasing their mothers. I assumed…"

"It's not about my mother. It has nothing to do with my mother." She fought the panicked edge in her voice.

"I'm sorry. I've upset you." He studied his menu. It wasn't his fault he'd hit a sore subject.

"My mother's dead," she blurted out.

He folded his menu and placed it on the table. "I am sorry. Truly."

The intensity of his eyes made her heart race. Why? Because she hadn't had good, solid male attention in a while?

"My mother died a long time ago." She recovered. "I don't like to talk about it."

"Then let's talk about something that will brighten your spirits. Have you ever been to London?"

"No."

"And she's not going now."

She glanced up to find Adam towering over their table.

"What are you doing here?" she said, horrified.

"I've come to help you. This man is not who he says he is."

Chapter 3

"Have we met?" Kadenshar asked. The intruder reeked of Ash scent and youthful bravado.

"You know we haven't."

"Kade Sharpe." He extended his hand. It would take but a quick handshake to determine this demon's age, his power. Kade suspected him a mere infant.

Instead the coward ignored Kade and addressed the girl.

"I've done some research." He pulled a chair to the two-person table. "Dee, there's no record of a Kade Sharpe working for London University. There's no record of him anywhere. He doesn't exist." He glared at Kade. "Whatever you want, you're not getting it from her."

"And what do *you* want, Mr…?"

"Adam Smith. And I want nothing but this girl's safety."

Sure, and Kade was an angel on holiday.

"Adam, stop it. Mr. Sharpe is a consultant," Destiny said. "Of course you wouldn't find him in the faculty listing at the university."

The Ash Demon narrowed his eyes at Kadenshar. "I don't trust him."

"Please," she said. "You're embarrassing me."

"I won't let this creep take advantage of you," he bellowed.

The girl's cheeks flushed pink. Her *friend* was creating a scene. Why? To convince her to leave with him?

"Shall we discuss your concerns outside?" Kade offered, fearing this young demon might do something foolish like use his powers in public.

Who had sent him? A faction of Ash Demon? After all, they didn't want Kade returning Destiny to the Cadre with her mind intact. They wanted to destroy her, they believed, to save themselves.

"Fine." Adam stood.

"No, you guys, don't," Destiny pleaded.

Kade wondered whether this clever demon had already worked his way into her heart. Did she have feelings for him?

As Kade watched Adam leave the restaurant, he

touched the girl's silk-clad shoulder. "It will be fine," he assured. "I will convince him my intentions are honorable. It will only take a few minutes."

The waitress approached the table with their champagne.

"Please," he said. "Start without me."

He let his fingers brush against her cheek. He couldn't help himself. Her eyes sparkled bright blue with desire. Of course, along with his touch, he'd sent her an image of how he'd kiss her breast, touching the tip with his warm, moist tongue, circling it, his ministrations making it peak with wanting.

"Don't be long," she said in a breathy sigh.

Oh, this *was* going to be easy.

As soon as he could rid himself of the petulant demon waiting outside. Kadenshar didn't have time for such trivialities. Fighting over a woman—ridiculous! And that's what this looked like—two men fighting for the affection of a woman. Or in this case, for possession of a woman.

Kadenshar shoved the door open and glanced into the empty parking lot. What—had the demon lost his nerve? No, he sensed the imp's presence. Kadenshar walked toward Alki Beach, speculating that the young demon craved a spectacular display. On the water, perhaps?

With an abrupt gust of wind, Kadenshar was jettisoned across the shoreline and slammed into the water. The frigid temperature of Puget Sound would render a mere human helpless in seconds. Kadenshar fought his mortal body's weakness and shot out of the water back to shore.

Adam laughed as he casually leaned against a park bench. "They won't let you back in the restaurant looking like a drowned rat."

"You lack the honor of a true Ash Demon." Kadenshar straightened, water soaking through his suit, droplets falling from his fingertips.

"At least my father wasn't a traitor." Adam flung his arms forward, his fingertips sending powerful bursts of wind against Kadenshar's chest. He flew back and slammed against the side of the restaurant.

Hopefully the girl was on her second glass of champagne. Seeing this interchange would make his job more complicated.

He needed simple. Needed to get back to his brother.

Standing, he brushed off his black pants and jacket, now caked in muddied sand.

"You don't want to spar with me, boy," he said.

"But I do."

Adam flung out his arms again but this time, with a mere narrowing of his eyes, Kade shot a bolt of black lightning to his adversary's chest. The demon fell to his knees, a closed fist clutching his shirt where the lightning had struck.

"There will be others," Adam said. "Many others."

Kade approached him. "There needn't be. I will take care of the girl and protect our kind."

"No, you are weak. You had the disease. You will fail and they know it."

"The Grigori sent you?" Kade's blood ran cold.

The demon smiled. "She is mine. It is meant to be."

He raised his hand in some attempt to attack yet again. Kade grabbed his wrist.

"Don't be a fool."

"You can't have her. I will do anything to keep you from having her."

"You've fallen in love with the girl?" Kade was horrified. The girl's inherent powers were so strong they had seduced an Ash Demon?

"Mr. Sharpe?" the girl called.

Distracted by her voice, Kade lost his concentration. Adam pummeled him in the chest and Kade catapulted across the beach. He hit the ground hard, his head slamming against a rock. Opening his eyes, he struggled to make out the blurred vision of his nemesis and his charge.

"Oh, my God, Adam! What have you done?" she cried.

"He's bad news, Dee. Come on, we have to go."

Kadenshar stood, wavered and narrowed his eyes.

"No, wait. No!" Dee called, trying to free herself from Adam's clutches.

"Do not do this!" Kadenshar ordered. He drew strength from deep in his chest. He'd need perfect calibration to accomplish his next move. With a deep breath, he shot a bolt of black lightning to the ground, sending its current toward the couple. They were tossed in the air, flying forward. Kadenshar apported to catch her before she hit the ground.

She was in his arms, breathing heavily, her rose quartz charm dancing against her neck with her panic.

"What happened?" She looked up into his eyes with such confusion.

A good time to escape.

"Your friend is jealous. We must go."

"Is Adam—"

"He'll be fine. But he will continue to badger us and you promised me this one evening to plead my case."

He carried her to the restaurant entrance, placed her on her feet and motioned for his driver.

"Please help our friend," Kade ordered the valet. "He's intoxicated and violent."

She strained to see the young demon's body lying motionless on the beach.

"I should stay and help him," she said.

"He'll be fine."

They got in the car and drove away.

"I still don't understand what happened," she said.

"Your boyfriend is very possessive."

"He's not my boyfriend."

"He fights like a man in love." He motioned to his wet clothes.

"My God, he did that?"

"As opposed to me choosing to go for a swim fully clothed?" he shot back. "Yes, he did this."

Idiot. Adam should have known better than to pick a fight with a superior Ash like Kadenshar. They had to have told him who he was up against.

They. Who were *they?*

Kadenshar wouldn't believe the Grigori had lost faith in him and sent this twit to do their bidding. The Grigori didn't work that way.

"I'm sorry."

He glanced at the girl, her eyes dimmed with regret.

"You have nothing to be sorry about." He wanted to touch her again but feared her essence might seduce him as it had young Adam. No, Kade was a seasoned, mature Ash Demon. He couldn't be manipulated by mortal lust or the ghastly emotion called love.

Something crashed against the back window, breaking the glass. She screamed and jumped toward the front seat as unforgiving hands clamped around Kadenshar's neck and yanked him out the back window, into the street. He heard the car screech to a stop, felt the howl of winds swirl around him, carrying him up and across the Sound, away from the bridge, away from the girl.

Who was this creature? Although young, Adam clearly must have spawned from strong seed.

No matter. This exercise was tiresome. And irritating.

Kade shot a lightning bolt to the earth and sailed straight down to within the car's reach. Adam was opening the back door. Kade grabbed him and hurled him across the lanes into oncoming traffic.

Kade looked inside his limousine.

Destiny cowered in the corner, her eyes round with terror.

"We have no time. You need to come with me," he said. He would have to tell her the truth, at least some of the truth.

"Now!" He grabbed her wrist and pulled her from the car, taking flight, soaring above the water toward the city where they could disappear amidst the mass of humanity.

His mortal body began to shake as it struggled to regulate the chill of the wind against his wet clothes. With his firm hold on her waist, they sailed across the water. She'd gone limp, apparently fainting again.

This was going to be the great crystal healer? He brought them down in a park near the Market, their bodies cloaked in black shadow to avoid unwanted attention. A homeless man glanced at them then closed his eyes and mumbled something under his breath. Other than the handful of homeless, the park was quiet and empty.

"Can you stand?" he asked, releasing her.

She opened her eyes. The blue had darkened with confusion and fear.

"I will not hurt you," he said.

"We flew."

"You are safe now."

"Adam jumped on the car…he…broke the glass…he pulled you out and…you flew."

"It's all right. My hotel is up Pine. We'll order room service and start this evening over."

"No, I can't." She stepped away from him and put out her hand. "I flew. It's not possible. Across water. Just now."

A few more steps back and she'd trip over their homeless friend.

"Professor Rue, you're exhausted," he started.

"I'm wet and cranky. Please, let's go to my hotel and—"

"No! My God, no!" She took off across the park. "Someone help me!"

"Professor!" he called, chasing after her. He couldn't very well fly in front of the audience that was forming. The frantic woman raced into the street. Satan's ghost, she was going to kill herself.

But if she died, so would his brother.

He apported to her side, grabbed her arm and snatched her out of the path of an oncoming car. "Stay out of the street. Are you mad?"

They stood in front of a wine shop. With a lost expression, she looked into his eyes and he heard her thoughts, one that troubled him more than the rest: *I'd rather die than go crazy.*

"You are not going crazy," he said in a low, soothing tone.

She blinked, her eyes not quite focused. He sensed his words had calmed her, if only for a few seconds.

Then police lights reflected off the storefront glass. "Please let go of the female, sir," a voice ordered through a megaphone of some kind.

More complications. He released her arm but she didn't move.

He held her gaze as he heard the officers approach.

"Ma'am? Is everything all right?" a police officer interrupted.

Kade wanted him gone.

A second officer shoved Kadenshar against the metal gate designed to protect the store. "Hands above your head. Hell, this guy's all wet. What have you been doing?"

"I had an accident."

"I flew," she offered.

Kadenshar closed his eyes. Wonderful. Now he'd have to break her out of a mental hospital.

"She's traumatized," Kadenshar offered.

"Yeah, because of you," the cop accused.

Kadenshar watched in the window's reflection as the other cop led Destiny to the backseat of the patrol car and kneeled to talk to her, treating her like a child.

The other cop smacked Kadenshar across the back of his head to get his attention. "Is this a domestic dispute or is there more to it?"

"My friend is not well."

"So you chase her into the street to straighten her out? Come on, try the truth."

"That is the truth."

"What did you do to her?"

Kade kept silent. They had already decided that he was a…what? A rapist?

Ash Demons never had to force a woman to have sex. Women usually begged.

The first cop joined them beside the building. "I called for an ambulance to take her to the hospital. You want to tell me what happened? She's not talking."

"We met today. I've been sent to recruit Professor Rue for my employer."

"And your employer is?"

"The Department of Anachronistic Research at London University." He hoped she wasn't in earshot of his mention of the department. He had planned to ease that bit of information into their dinner conversation.

"What the hell is *anachronistic?*"

"They're a scientific group," Kade said.

"Yeah, for what?"

"You'd have to ask them. I'm a recruiter. Professor Rue is an expert in the field of brain study."

"What a crock." He shot Kadenshar a perturbed look and glanced at the squad car. "Goddamn it, she's gone!"

Had to get away. Had to escape.

Destiny raced up the street, her face wet with tears, her hands cold from the chill.

She'd confessed that she'd flown.

She knew what came next.

They'd take her to the hospital. She'd be locked up like Mom.

Clutching her purse tightly against her rib cage, she focused on getting away, becoming invisible. Finding safety.

Which was where? She couldn't escape her own mind, the hideousness that had been developing over the years: her mental prison.

Sprinting down an alley to elude police, a sob choked from her chest when she realized that she couldn't run from the insanity. Thirty was the magic number, which meant in three weeks she'd be completely cracked. She wouldn't know who she was, wouldn't remember her name or recognize her friends. She wouldn't know what to call sunshine and would forget the name of her favorite city, Seattle.

If she was like her mom, she had weeks, maybe only days to live before it was all lost. What would she do?

She'd wanted to start her research on neutralizing brain transmitters, thereby giving people with mental disorders another chance.

Giving herself a chance.

It seemed as though her chances were up.

She eyed the pink door of a popular restaurant and heard music and laughter echo from the other side. She clung firmly to her purse, wishing she could pause and pull out her amethyst point. It was purple and calming and felt solid in her hand. They'd found it in Mom's belongings at the hospital, one of the few things she'd taken with her, one of many stones her father had gifted to Dee.

Had he known the direction her life would take? That she'd lose her mind like Mom? Is that why he'd kept his distance?

She opened the pink door and was assaulted by the sound of laughter and music. She needed to escape inside, find the bathroom and get her wits back.

What she had left of them.

Someone grabbed her arm. "Are you okay?" Adam said.

But how? He'd been tossed across two lanes of traffic on the West Seattle Bridge. He couldn't have survived, couldn't have known where she'd be or gotten here so quickly. Unless more time had passed than she realized. The mental illness was taking over, stealing time as well as her sanity.

He pulled her away from the door.

Adam. Adam was okay. He'd always been nice to her, baking her brownies on the weekends, bringing her candy he'd pick up from various parts of the world. He knew her weak spot—sweets. He knew a lot about her. He was a good friend.

Would he remain her friend when he found out the truth?

With a firm hand he led her out of the restaurant and down the alley. They ducked into an alcove used for putting out trash.

"You're okay?" he said. "I'm so glad."

"But you— You were thrown into traffic. That man…he…we flew and…"

"Shhh." He held her against his chest and stroked her hair. "What happened to Mr. Sharpe?" he asked.

"The police. I think they arrested him. They were going to take me, too."

He looked into her eyes. "What? Why?"

"To the hospital. I'm losing my mind."

There, she'd let it out.

Adam smiled. "No, you're not losing your mind. You're tired, but you're okay."

Her body nearly went limp with relief. Adam was here. He'd take care of her. He said she wasn't losing her mind. And she wanted to believe him.

"I wouldn't be able to survive if something bad happened to you," he said.

He caressed her cheek with his fingertips and she closed her eyes. Relaxing. Everything would be okay. She could trust Adam. She knew him. Not like Mr. Sharpe. A stranger. He flew. They'd flown.

"Dee," Adam whispered, then kissed her.

The desperate kiss tasted bitter and tart.

She pushed at his chest. "Adam?"

He pressed his lips to hers to silence her protest. Crazy. She was crazy. Adam would never force himself on her. Never do something this offensive.

She slapped him, hoping it would wake her up from this nightmare.

He grinned at her. "I never thought you'd like it rough."

He slapped her back. Although not hard, it shocked her out of her trance. She kicked, trying to hit something crucial. He was too damned strong.

"I want it, too, baby," he muttered against her hair.

Pulled closer, she could feel him grow hard. She was going to be sick. She'd never been attracted to this man, never enjoyed his touch, even in friendship.

"No!" she protested, turning her face and looking for something to bite. She found his arm and bit down.

He cried out—but not in pain.

He liked it?

He managed to unzip her dress, frantically trying to loosen it from her body.

"This isn't real. You're not doing this," she said. The only way to survive was to hope this was part of her sickness.

"I've wanted you forever. We belong together."

She punched and squirmed. She wouldn't let him take this from her. Her dignity. Her sanity.

"Adam, snap out of it!"

She stomped on his foot, thankful she'd chosen to wear high heels. He loosened his grip and she kneed him in the crotch. When he stumbled backward she took off but lost her footing on the uneven brick. She staggered to the ground, scraping her knees.

Adam came up behind her and clamped an arm around her waist. "So beautiful, so very beautiful."

"Adam, stop!" She pinched her eyes shut, wishing this hallucination away, begging God for the ability to create good fantasies instead of hellish ones.

"Please, God," she whispered.

"You mean *please, demon,*" he whispered against her ear.

She realized she'd take insanity over this kind of horror any day, because this wasn't a hallucination.

She was being molested in a dark alley by one of her best friends.

Chapter 4

Kadenshar had never wanted to kill a fellow demon more than he wanted to kill this rat bastard. As Adam nuzzled her shoulder and pressed himself against her, Kade grabbed him by the neck and tossed him across the alley. The juvenile demon hit the brick wall and fell to the ground. His human form lay motionless on the wet pavement.

But he wouldn't lie still for long. Kade sensed the demon had lost his mind over the woman, seduced by the temptress called Destiny. Could the demon have been seduced by the very thing he was supposed to tempt mortals with—her inherent power?

Or was it worse: had he fallen in love with the fragile creature?

Destiny lay on the wet pavement half-naked, trembling. Pathetic. She couldn't even protect herself, much less influence mystical forces of dark and mortal realms.

The young demon stirred. It would be his choice, but Kade sensed the boy would fight until one of them lost. Completely.

Kade didn't want to destroy him, just remove him from the equation.

An equation that was meant to be simple and easy.

"Sssshhheeee's mine!" Adam howled, springing to his feet and fisting his hands.

No, not simple. Complicated. Kade would have to destroy one of his own to save a mortal. Bile seared the back of his throat.

"Back down, boy," Kade warned. "There are bigger issues here than you and I fighting over a girl."

"I won't let you hurt her." He crept like a panther toward the girl.

"I don't intend to hurt her."

"Liar!"

The girl's shoulders jerked with his shout.

The light mist turned into thick, wet droplets of rain slapping at Kade's face, pounding against the girl's body as she lay trembling on the ground. Kade must get her to safety, warm her before the chill broke down her defenses, causing her illness…possibly death.

No, Tendaeus was depending on him.

"I'm on a mission," Kade said. "For all of us."

"And I'm on a mission for me!" Adam lunged at the girl.

Kade apported between them and knocked the boy to the ground. "I don't want to do this," he warned.

A tunnel of wind sucked Kadenshar into its vortex, but it wasn't strong enough to pull him away from his adversary. Adam's skill had been weakened by his lust for the girl. The anticipation of coupling with her had diluted the boy's power, making him more mortal than Ash.

Disgusting.

"You want her so badly you'd risk being destroyed?" Kade asked.

The boy's eyes radiated defiance. "It is you that will be destroyed."

Lightning sparked across the murky Seattle sky. A deafening crack of thunder followed and the girl shrieked. Adam was growing stronger.

"I will have her!" He stood and the winds picked up speed, swirling around Kade. He felt his body lift off the ground.

A smile curled the boy's lips, his gaze drifting to the helpless girl. If he wasn't stopped Adam would bury his seed inside the Crystal Goddess and she would undoubtedly go mad after being violated by a dear friend.

Ash Demons would be safe from her powers.

And Tendaeus would be dead.

The wind wrapped around his chest, driving him away from Adam. No. He would not lose this fight.

From his demon core, Kade leveled a bolt of black lightning at the human heart of his adversary. The boy cried out, the sparkle in his eyes flickering, then fading to black. The color of mortal death.

The wind ceased and Kade stumbled backward, getting his balance. When the young demon's body was found, the external wound would have healed and it would appear he'd died of heart failure.

A whimpering sound drew his attention to the girl. Disgust filled his chest. Because of her, this weak creature that was responsible for Kade's invisible chains, he had destroyed one of his own.

She hadn't seen what happened. If she had, she'd be lost to him completely. As it was, he was going to have a difficult time explaining tonight's events.

"Dr. Rue," he said, kneeling beside her. He started to pull her to her feet, careful to turn her away from her dead friend.

Stumbling to a darkened corner of the alley, she retched. He gathered her purse and went to her, placing a hand on her shoulder. She pressed her cheek against the brick building as if wanting to absorb its strength.

"Your dress," he said. She absently let him adjust it and zip it up. She clutched her purse to her chest.

He gave her space, a few minutes to get a hold of herself. But they couldn't linger. Other Ash could be close, wanting their turn at the girl. Their turn to drive her mad.

He placed his arm around her shoulders and led

her out of the alley. She didn't even attempt to look at her friend.

Something was wrong. Typical human compassion would compel her to inquire about the boy. But then, she wasn't normal or he wouldn't be on this mission to bring her to the Cadre. Still, he found it difficult to accept that this female was the great hope for peace and balance between their worlds. She was utterly weak and defenseless.

Which is probably why they sent you for this horrid job. They knew Kadenshar was considered the great Ash leader, the one who used intelligence instead of emotion to dictate his strategies. He was strong enough to protect Destiny from a gang of Ash and their mind tricks. This girl would go insane within hours without Kade's help.

"My hotel is around the corner," he said.

She walked beside him but didn't speak.

"Professor?" He hesitated and studied her eyes. They looked empty, as if the terror had stripped her ability to reason. He touched her cheek, hoping the heat from his fingertips would warm her back to consciousness.

Instead her eyes rolled back and she withered like a faerie ribbon dropped from the reel. With one arm behind her knees, he scooped her up and carried her toward the inn.

She had fainted twice in one day, which worried him. How was this frail thing going to become a great Crystal Goddess and save his brother?

With an eye scanning the shadows, he made the three-block trek to the inn. He walked through the lobby and nodded politely to the woman behind the desk.

"Her first experience with champagne," he said in explanation.

The woman smiled and refocused on her computer screen.

The inn was quiet. Excellent. He didn't want witnesses to his presence. The police would no doubt be looking for him since he'd apported from their clutches. He didn't easily blend in thanks to his long hair and powerful demeanor.

Powerful to mortals, ordinary to fellow demons.

When he didn't pass any guests on the way to the room, he took a deep breath of relief. They'd be safe for the present.

Unlocking the door with his mind skill, he breezed into the room and laid the girl on the cushioned bed. Covering her with blankets, he touched her forehead. She burned.

At least she was alive.

He stripped off his muddied clothes and eyed his selection of silk boxer shorts.

A soft squeak drew his attention to the bed. Turning onto her side, she blinked her eyes open. She stared at him blankly.

A perverse part of him hoped his nakedness, his size, would shock her back to reality.

"Dr. Rue?" he said.

She blinked. Stared. Said nothing.

Apparently she had sunk too deep into her own misery to appreciate what he had to offer.

He slipped on silk boxers and went to the bathroom for a hotel robe. No sense getting dressed when all he was going to do was play nurse to a weak girl.

A shame. He'd hoped for more: flirtation, seduction and consummation. At the least, relief for his human maleness. He wouldn't enjoy mating with this female, but his body would welcome the satisfaction, the dominance.

Yes, he thought, splashing water on his slightly bearded face, he would dominate her to control her. But how when she was barely lucid?

He tied the belt on his robe loosely. His best skills were those of seduction and mating. He had gained much experience from his visits to the mortal realm for recreation and entertainment. And he'd completely satisfied the females he'd bedded. They would never bed another without seeing Kadenshar's green eyes looking back at them. He'd left his demon essence inside of many, although his kind did not need them to bridge to the mortal realm. Ash Demon were a highly evolved species, one created to tempt humans with their own delusions of grandeur.

The females he'd bedded felt grand indeed after one night with Kadenshar.

But seduce a barely functioning sorceress?

Kade walked back into the room, but the bed was

empty. She was outside on the balcony, leaning against the railing as if intending to jump.

"Dr. Rue!" In a flash he was at her side. He grabbed hold of her waist as she started to lean over the metal rail. "What in the devil's name are you doing?"

Scooping her in his arms, he went the bed, his heart pounding against his chest with panic. She'd been trying to kill herself?

He sat her on the bed.

"I must die."

He froze at her admission.

Desperation colored her bright blue eyes. "Can you kill me?"

His fingers sprang free of her shoulder. "You're talking nonsense."

"I can't live if I am—" she paused "—insane."

So she had enough of her senses back to realize that nothing that had happened tonight made logical sense. Therefore, the only explanation was that she'd gone mad.

"We should clean you up." He shot her a tender smile. "That will make you feel better." He led her to the bathroom, sat her on the toilet seat and proceeded to dampen a washcloth. He wouldn't leave her presence, not while she considered doing herself harm.

Selfish girl. Even if she didn't know about her potential as a Crystal Goddess, what about her scientific abilities? Was she going to throw that away because she thought she was going mad? Surely she was thinking of no one but herself.

"Why did Adam hurt me?" she choked.

"Shhh." He reached down to wipe dirt from her cheek. "He must have drunk too much. He had a crush on you and it got the better of him."

"No, we were friends."

A male and a female friends? Not possible.

"He… What happened?" she asked.

Kade tipped her chin to look into his eyes. Using demon influence to convince her everything was fine, he said, "We resolved our conflict. There is nothing more to worry about."

"The voices." She blinked, her eyes growing wide.

"What voices?"

"Don't you hear them?" She eyed the far corner of the bathroom.

Were Ash Demons taunting her with their whispers of devilish horrors? Or had this evening's trauma destroyed her sanity after all?

"There's no one here but you and I, Destiny. You are safe."

She looked up at him. The fear in her eyes warmed to trust, but he would not allow himself to feel anything for this girl, his enemy.

Wrapping her arms around his waist, she sighed and held on to him. He reached down to stroke her hair and caught himself. Starting at his reflection in the mirror, a bitter taste filled his mouth. He'd nearly been lured by the seductress called compassion.

He hadn't felt it since…no, not even when his

brother and his father were killed. That had been rage, followed by self-loathing that tore at his demon heart when he heard his mother's howls of grief.

Ash Demons were cursed, to be sure, allowed to feel what mortals feel: to fall in love, to experience pity.

He eyed Destiny, who clung to him the way moss clings to the great weeping willows of the enchanted St. Yve Wood. The girl trembled as her whimpers of fear echoed against the tile walls.

Cadre leaders were convinced this was the girl who could bring order and balance to the mortal and dark realms? Kade could hardly believe it.

It didn't matter. His main concern was freeing his brother from the crystal prison. They claimed to need a Crystal Goddess to successfully free Tendaeus. It made no sense. Kade knew of adepts like Lady Aurora Maybank and Mersey Bane, the shapeshifting feline. Surely they had the ability to release his brother.

Which meant this assignment was a manipulation to get the girl safely back to St. Yve. Who better to anticipate the tricks of Ash Demons than an Ash himself?

With teary bright blue eyes, she looked up and said, "Please take me to the hospital."

"Are you physically wounded?"

"No, but my mind—" Her voice caught.

"You're exhausted and upset by your friend's behavior. You need to rest. Sit back and let me finish cleaning your face."

With each stroke of the washcloth he sensed her fear dissolve into trust. Devastated and broken, she was most vulnerable to him—a perfect opportunity to gain favor with her…and influence.

He finished cleaning the dirt off her face, then kneeled and lifted her dress to wipe at her scraped knees. She laid her head against his shoulder.

Saint's ghost, she was making him come alive with need. No, he couldn't risk seducing her and scaring her into a deeper state of panic.

"Come." He stood and grabbed the other robe off the bathroom door. "You need to sleep." When she didn't move, he took her hand and led her to the bed. She absently sat on the edge, hugging her midsection.

"Your dress is wet," he said. "Let's wrap you in something warm." He motioned to the robe in his hand.

She didn't move, didn't look at him.

"I will help." He placed the robe on the bed and unfolded her arms.

Her blank expression snapped up to meet his eyes.

"I won't hurt you," he said. "But we must get you out of these wet clothes."

With steady hands, he reached around to unzip her dress.

"A good night's rest is what you need," he whispered. "We'll sort it out in the morning."

Once unzipped, he trailed the dress off her shoulders and down. She stood, letting it fall to the floor.

That's when he noticed the black lace bra and

panties. Had she worn them especially for him? Because he guessed this uptight scientist wouldn't routinely wear something as sexy as black lace.

"The voices," she whispered, closing her eyes. "Make them stop."

"Shhh, you're going to be fine."

He would give her a special bedtime drink flavored with venenum. He'd brought the potion in case she resisted his charm and refused to accompany him to England.

As he draped the robe across her shoulders, his hand grazed her skin. It was soft and warm, humming with a vibration that made him ache to touch more of her.

Kade realized she *did* have some kind of bewitching power to make him want to take her so freely.

Focus, he scolded himself. *Focus on freeing your brother.*

Only, could he remove her undergarments and still resist her charms?

Destiny leaned into this stranger with the warm, gentle hands and pretended he was her boyfriend, her lover, a man sworn to protect her from all that was evil in the world.

Adam had attacked her? No, she couldn't believe it. But the only alternative was she'd gone crazy.

Panic squeezed her chest.

"Take a deep breath," Mr. Sharpe said as if he sensed her anxiety.

She felt him release the clasp of her bra. With his fingertip, he slipped one strap off her shoulder.

Gentle, so very gentle.

The other strap slid off her shoulder, exposing her naked breasts. They felt heavy with wanting as she leaned into this man. Her nipples brushed against his terry-cloth robe and peaked with need. His hands—she wanted his hands on her breasts, massaging, squeezing.

God, she'd lost her mind completely to crave this stranger's touch.

"Destiny," he whispered.

Her heart raced as he traced her spine with his fingertips, down to the base and up again, trailing his fingers to the side and around the front to brush against the curve of her breast.

A throbbing sensation started low, between her legs. She wanted more. Needed more.

Standing, she struggled to breathe against the assault of desire.

"What do you want?" he whispered against her ear.

She wanted this man inside her, filling her with his strength, with hope.

She untied his robe and pressed her bare skin against his. Heat burned low. The ache between her legs grew unbearable, painful.

Her world was chaos, and the only thing she knew for sure was that she wanted this stranger inside her, now, for as long as possible.

That's all that mattered.

She studied his face, his set jaw and fiery green eyes. Eyes filled with passion, with intense need that matched her own.

Closing her eyes, she leaned forward to kiss him.

"No."

His deep, rich voice shocked her eyes open. With firm hands to her shoulders, he held her at a distance. His eyes no longer radiated desire.

Anger flashed across the dark green. "I will get you something to drink."

He turned to the bathroom and left her standing there, naked except for her panties. The frigid chill of reality shot goose bumps down her arms. She rubbed them.

She was losing her mind. What else would explain throwing herself at a stranger she'd only met this afternoon? A man who could have furthered her career?

What kind of career could a mad scientist truly hope for?

A mad scientist. Yes, that's what she was.

He came out of the bathroom and handed her a half-full glass of brown liquid. Probably hundred-proof scotch.

"I don't drink," she said.

"You need to drink this. Trust me."

Trust him? She'd nearly *jumped* him.

She took the glass, suddenly self-conscious of her nakedness. With a placid expression he pulled her robe closed and tied the sash.

Tight.

"Go on, drink," he encouraged.

"I'm—" She glanced at the washed-out carpet, then up to his eyes. "I'm sorry. About what just happened."

"You've been through an ordeal this evening," he said as if to explain away her inappropriate behavior.

She took a sip from the glass, surprised by its sweetness. "What is this?"

"A special blend from home," he said, sitting in a thick-cushioned chair across the room.

"Where's home?"

An odd smile curled his lips. Pleasant but pained.

"Finish your drink and sleep," he said. "We have a long journey ahead."

"You...you still want me?"

She'd meant as a scientist, but the inference hung between them.

Did he want her as a woman?

"Yes," he said. "Definitely."

Her nipples hardened again.

"I'm nuts," she said.

"Don't say that."

"I think that I flew across Seattle and was attacked by my best friend. And I forced myself on you just now."

"You've been traumatized," he explained. "That combined with your medical condition—"

"Mental condition."

"I meant your low blood sugar issues."

"Low blood sugar does not explain the voices."

He leaned forward in his chair, cupping his glass

with firm, masculine hands. Those same hands she'd ached to have touch her breasts.

"What do the voices say?" he asked.

"You're mocking me."

"No. Please tell me."

She sighed, quieted herself and struggled to make sense of the whispers.

"Crazy woman…insane like her mother," she repeated. *"You will kill, like your mother."*

She opened her eyes and downed the rest of her drink, placing the glass on the nightstand.

"What does that mean?" he asked. "Kill like your mother?"

"It means I'm crazy. My mother never killed anyone, she couldn't kill anyone. She was locked up in a mental hospital."

"I see."

"I need to see a doctor."

"We'll talk about it in the morning." He set his glass on top of the television. "Get comfortable. I'll tuck you in."

She climbed beneath the soft linen. The adrenaline must have worn off, because a sudden wave of exhaustion blanketed her as surely as the bedding he tucked around her body.

She felt safe, cocooned. She reached up and touched the stone around her neck. Another treasure from a mother she never knew. The rose quartz crystal with amethyst accent gave her hope that she would, someday, be loved.

"Where did you get it?" He sat beside her on the bed.

"It was my mother's."

"Rose quartz." He hesitated. "The love stone."

For someone who had never been loved, she thought.

You don't deserve to be loved. You deserve to suffer.

"God, please make it stop," she whispered, rubbing the rose quartz with her thumb.

"The voices?" he asked.

She nodded, horrified that another human being knew about the family illness she feared would consume her.

Yet the voices stopped when Mr. Sharpe spoke to her, his voice somehow having the power to clear the craziness from her brain.

"Sleep now," he said.

As if under his spell, she sighed and drifted off. The entire evening seemed like a bad dream conjured by her fear of turning into her mother.

Her mother. Dee had often dreamed of her, the red-haired beauty with an infectious smile and generosity of spirit. But tonight her mind drifted away from thoughts of Mom.

Dee pictured herself standing in the middle of an enchanted forest, surrounded by elegant weeping willows, alder and silver birch trees. A beautiful creature with gossamer lavender wings and jewel-toned eyes floated up to Destiny.

"The princess has joined us. Come play, come dance," the faerie invited.

Behind the creature Dee could see faeries of every shape and color join hands, dancing with merriment and abandon.

"Join us! Join us!" they sang to the sounds of tinkling music that filled the forest.

"Next time," Dee said with a smile.

Her heart was being called to the forest's edge. Following a path illuminated with a soft orange glow, she hiked past a sparkling pool of water that emanated a magical mist. It looked warm and inviting. She'd have to visit this spot again, when she could linger, but right now she sensed the importance of forging ahead. When she reached the clearing, she gasped at the sight of a majestic castle surrounded by a lawn of vibrant green. Tall windows punctuated the rich stone walls; well-crafted gargoyles seemed so real their wings fluttered with the sense of her presence.

They would protect her. This would be her home.

She would be a princess after all, revered and respected. Maybe even loved.

Foolish, stupid girl, the voices taunted.

No, she would not let the voices invade her dreams. Focus on the castle, on the warm sunshine penetrating the clouds and caressing her skin.

She raised her arms to the sky and tipped her face to the nourishing sun. But the warmth faded as a dark black cloud passed overhead, blocking the sun's loving light.

Her arms felt heavy and she collapsed, sitting cross-legged on the damp grass. The bright green beneath her faded to gray. Her gaze drifted to her wrists. They were shackled in black stone bracelets. On her middle finger she wore a ring with an oval grayish stone with streaks of green.

You wear shackles on your wrists. You are our prisoner.

"No!" she cried, struggling to remove the bracelets. They were tight, no clasp, no way to free herself.

Don't fret, my sweet. Take this.

A knife appeared in her hand. She slipped it between her skin and the bracelet on her left hand.

Cut it off.

With a jerk, she snapped the bracelet free from her wrist, the black stones tumbling to the earth.

That's right. Now the other.

She pressed the knife to her skin and slid it beneath the bracelet. But this one was tighter, and she wasn't using her dominant hand.

They will kill you if you don't free yourself!

She jerked the knife and the second bracelet came free. The round stones shot across her lap, staining her beige pants bright red.

Red? No. The stones were black, they were—

Her pulse pounded against her eardrums. Blood. Oozing from her wrist. She'd cut herself by accident.

By accident? Hardly, the voices taunted.

She pressed her hand against the wound, but blood seeped between her fingers.

Stupid, weak girl.

Laughter echoed from the forest, drifting up to her, swirling around her head like bees swarming a hive. Menacing laughter of many, a crowd, all laughing at her death.

"No." She stood, wavered, and someone grabbed her arm to steady her.

The laugher of her enemies competed with that of one deep male voice. She looked up into Mr. Sharpe's cold green eyes.

"Stupid, weak girl."

Kade glanced up from his book and eyed the girl. She'd never make it through the night.

And he surely wouldn't, not with her moaning and crying out, writhing in pain. Or was it something else? Was she having a sexual dream about mating with Kadenshar?

"Ah, don't flatter yourself," he muttered.

More likely, the Ash rebels were at it again, filling her dreams with horror. Yet his potion should have numbed her mind to their influence. He'd used it on other mortals to influence and control.

But she wasn't a typical mortal. Her inbred powers meant her chemical makeup was not like that of any other creature on this planet.

She was a healer, a would-be Crystal Goddess.

"Let me go," she moaned.

A would-be goddess that was powerless to defend herself.

Kade shut his book and went to the sliding door, stepping onto the small balcony. Breathing in the night air, he ignored the desperate pleas from his female companion.

He'd given her the potion. There was nothing more he could do.

Not entirely true. He could dig through that purse of hers and see if she had any other remedies. Valium, perhaps? Other mind-numbing drugs?

He suspected she'd wanted them, wanted something to stop the nightmares. The potion should have knocked her out, but it seemed to have a limited effect on the would-be healer.

A sudden flash of light slammed him against the glass door. Not one but four Demon soldiers stood over him, two pinning him to the glass.

The leader glanced into the room, then back at Kade. "Thank you, Kadenshar. We'll take the girl now."

Chapter 5

Kade was immobilized by an invisible force that pinned his wrists and waist to the glass. They must be Grigori soldiers.

Not good.

Grigori ruled the dark realm. They decided how conflicts and problems would be dealt with. Is that what they considered Kade? A problem?

He had to buy time, regain his strength from the sudden blow. He knew the soldiers were weak-minded, that they followed orders of the Grigori—but could be influenced by other, stronger demons.

Like a modern Ash.

"What does Grigori plan to do with her?" Kade asked as calmly as possible.

The lead soldier took a step closer. His rancid breath smelled of stale fish. They were hideous creatures, their faces gray and wrinkled with deep-set orange eyes that could burn if you held their gaze.

They were meant to be menacing, but right now the only thing Kadenshar feared was losing his brother.

"It doesn't matter what they plan for her," the soldier said, eyeing Kade as if he'd never seen an Ash Demon in human form. "The Grigori wants her back."

He motioned to one of his men, who passed Kade and went inside. Glancing over his shoulder, Kade watched the dull-witted soldier stalk to the bed— slowly, as if he feared the girl.

You couldn't reason with Grigori soldiers. Once given an order they were like vampires with their fangs into mortal flesh.

Kade needed to seduce them away from the girl. What tool could he use? Ah, a thought struck. *Fear.*

"I wouldn't touch her," Kade warned. "See the crystal around her neck? She only needs to utter the spell and you will be sucked into her charm and held prisoner for all of eternity. You've heard the stories."

The leader snapped his attention to Kade.

"I've only learned of her power since I've spent time with her," Kade said. "The Grigori couldn't have known the extent of her talents."

"You are toying with me, Ash," he said.

"Am I? There is nothing worse than being locked in that crystal chamber. And she'll wear you like a frivolous bauble."

The leader glanced at Destiny. His soldier was pulling the covers down, off her body. His eyes burned with lust. Grigori guards didn't get much, sexually speaking. They were too damned ugly.

"I want some of that," a second guard said, sounding like a child.

"If you touch her, she will awaken," Kade warned. "She will capture all of you."

The leader licked his lips, obviously torn between wanting sexual release and wanting to live. He suddenly pressed the tip of his blade to Kade's neck.

"Do you lie to me, Ash?"

"On my life, I tell you the truth."

It was the truth, to a degree. She would eventually be able to capture and detain paras, interrogate them, destroy them.

Annihilate the Ash race, if she so desired.

But right now she was nothing more than a limp human female about to be violated. With his armored hand, the soldier coaxed her terry-cloth robe down, off her shoulder, exposing the curve of her breast.

It's not that Kade cared what they did to her. Her needy blue eyes hadn't affected him before when she'd nearly kissed him.

Yet he couldn't stand the thought of those brutal Grigori guards violating her against her will. And

what if she awakened? She'd be traumatized beyond recovery.

"I wouldn't," Kade warned the soldier whose
eyes had grown wide with wanting.

Kade took a deep breath and focused on getting
into the girl's thoughts. If he could control her, ter-
rorize her into waking up and crying out…

Kade would manifest a safe environment, then
strip it from the girl. He created a loving scene in
her mind: Destiny swinging carelessly in a play-
ground. Her mother strolled up the walk, calling her
name. The girl jumped from the swing and went to
her mother's loving embrace.

Suddenly they stood in front of an ominous white
building. The mother was being dragged away. The
little girl cried out, screamed for her mother.

Pain, he could feel Destiny's pain. The little girl
held out her arms…her mother was pulled away…
the mother broke free and raced to her little girl but
passed right by her, terror filling her eyes as she ran
into the street, into the headlights of a moving car.
Her body sailed through the air, landing against the
pavement.

Landing at the feet of Kade's own father and
brother. The deafening sound of a P-Cell blaster
shook Kade from his dream.

"Devil's tears!" Kade gasped as Destiny simul-
taneously cried out.

This woman *was* powerful. She had somehow
turned her own nightmare into Kade's.

"Stand back!" the lead soldier ordered.

"Mama! Mama, no!" Destiny said, sitting up in bed and grabbing her charm.

"Kill her!" the leader ordered.

"Grigori wants her alive!" Kade shouted.

"She will destroy us," he argued.

"I can protect you. I am the only one who can protect paras from this girl. I can control her."

"A demon's word is but a mirage," the lead soldier said.

He eyed Destiny, who flopped back against the bed, exhausted from the mental torture. A soldier pointed his blade against her partially naked chest.

"If you kill her, we will all suffer."

The leader's gaze snapped up to Kade's. Hot—red-hot—burning Kade's eyes.

"I would not lie to agents of Grigori," Kade said.

A para would be destroyed for such an atrocity.

The lead soldier broke the staring contest. Kade blinked, struggling to get his vision back.

"So be it," the leader said. He pointed his sword at his second in command. "Watch her. Do not harm her. Do not violate her. We will be back."

We?

A surge of electricity spiked through Kade's body as he was catapulted off the balcony, soaring across the city. The soldier held him by the neck, cutting off air.

"The ley lines cross there!"

They plummeted down and crossed over.

Kade slammed against something hard and unyielding. He opened his eyes and found himself in the Grigori Temple, sprawled across stone steps that led to the altar. The Grigori council loomed above, their expressions hard and angry.

"You dare to use your Ash Demon mind influence to change the course of this guard's mission?"

Breathe. He had to get air in his lungs so he could speak. He rolled over and got to his feet.

Whack! Something pummeled him in the back and he went facedown to the steps.

"You kneel before Grigori," a voice said from behind him.

He glanced over his shoulder: Pagroe. Power-hungry bastard. Probably trying to court favor with the Grigori by proving Kade a traitor. Pagroe wielded a whip in one hand and a mallet in the other.

"Don't look at me. Look at your masters!" He snapped the whip, slicing across Kade's naked back. He'd lost his robe in the flight to the dark realm.

Kade ground his teeth and snapped his attention to the council.

Grigori were hard, obstinate creatures bent on maintaining order in the dark realm, even if that meant destroying their own.

"We don't trust your kind." The Chief Council stepped down from the altar. "Too many human tendencies, too much arrogance." The creature towered over Kade. He was taller than the rest, about eight feet in height, looking more dragon-like than human.

Kade did not look into his eyes. The submissive act might give him the opening he needed to plead his case.

"If the girl dies now the vibrational fabric will be torn and the damage will devastate our kind," Kade said. He had to make this bigger than the mission to free his brother.

"Our kind? You mean Ash Demon," the Chief Council said.

"Not just Ash. She can not die by our hand or we risk complete destruction of our world."

"I did not send my guard to kill her."

"But he was about to when I stopped him."

The Chief Council eyed his servant.

"She was going to crystallize us, master."

"Fool, she is not a skilled adept. Not yet." He eyed Kade. "You are a master manipulator, Kaden-shar."

"It doesn't take mastery to influence a guard."

Whack! The mallet slammed against his ribs.

"Say thank you when Grigori compliments your skill," Pagroe ordered.

"Thank you," Kade choked out.

"Enough." The Chief Council put up his hand. He kneeled and clenched Kade's jaw, tipping his face up. "How did you find out about the female?"

"The Cadre."

"You work with the Cadre?" His voice boomed.

"Not with them, master. You favor me as Ash leader because of my skill. I am presently manipulating the Cadre to gain access to their headquarters, where they are holding my brother."

"We cannot be concerned with the troubles of one over the well-being of many."

"True. But if I gain access to the Cadre, think of the power we will have. And if I save my brother, the strength of two leaders is that much stronger than that of one. His existence will bring even more power to the dark realm."

"We sense dissidence among the Ash regarding this matter."

"That is why you need Tendaeus," Kade said. "He is a fierce warrior."

"And you?"

"I am but your servant, my lord."

Another slash across his back. Kade ground his teeth against the mortal pain of his flesh being sliced open.

"Do not mock us, Kadenshar," the Chief Council said.

"I do not. I exist to fulfill my purpose, to tempt the human ego and encourage mortals to self-destruct. If you choose me to lead, then I will follow your directive with humility."

"And the Crystal Goddess, the one who is said to have more power than all the forces of the dark realm combined?"

He carefully raised his head to look into the eyes of the Chief Council. "She is presently a broken, pathetic creature. I will dominate her and free all our kind from imprisonment. Think of the possibilities if I control her power."

"If you fail—"

"I will not."

"If you do…" He paused.

"I will be destroyed. I understand."

"No." He paused. "You will become mortal. You will suffer pain and compassion. You will die a slow, torturous death."

"Yes, master."

Never to see his brother again…to exist in the disgrace of being mortal, weak and repulsive.

Never to experience the thrill of tempting a mortal ego, controlling a female's desire to bed him.

"Take him back!"

When Kade awakened, he wondered if they hadn't already started the transformation process from demon to mortal. His body ached from his head to his feet. His back throbbed from the thrashing of Pagroe's whip.

Everything ached except his cock, which swelled with an enormous erection. He felt someone press against his body. He opened his eyes. Destiny, hair tossed about her cheeks, slept peacefully with an arm flung across his groin.

No wonder he was hard.

And she was naked.

Had the Grigori cast some spell on him to make love to the girl? If so, would she have lost some of her potential powers because he'd buried his demon seed inside of her?

No, Grigori guards must have played this joke on him, trying to embarrass him by having him wake up naked next to the girl. They'd been shamed in front of their masters. It surprised him they hadn't done worse. But still…

Eyeing her sweet curves and fine skin, a part of him grew furious at the thought of the ugly creatures touching her. They weren't worthy of such beauty.

Heathens wake, what are you thinking of now?

He slipped out of bed and stood under an ice-cold shower, letting the water wash clean the blood from his lashings.

A vile curse, living in a mortal's body.

A curse he may never shake if he didn't satisfy the Grigori's demands.

I will dominate her and free all our kind from imprisonment. Think of the possibilities if I control her power.

Yes, it was the right course: dominate the girl and use her both to satisfy the Grigori and to free his brother.

With a groan, he stepped out of the shower, dried off and went into the bedroom. It was then he noticed the time. One in the afternoon. No mortal should sleep this long.

With a towel around his waist, he went to her bedside.

"Destiny?" he said, running the back of his

fingers across her cheek. "Destiny, it's time to wake up."

It's time to get moving and end this nightmare. He gripped her shoulder and gave her a gentle shake.

When she opened her eyes, an ominous chill snaked down his spine. Her normally bright blue eyes were gray, lifeless. Yet she breathed and she blinked. She was alive.

But was her mind?

He pulled the blankets to her chin. She looked so damn cold.

Pacing to the balcony door, he considered the possibility that the Ash night terrors had destroyed her mind. Or had she retreated to a place where they couldn't reach her?

Whatever the case, he had to figure out a way to bring her back. Yet he knew nothing about mortal healing, and she was still more mortal than Crystal Goddess.

He picked up his cell phone and placed an international call to Cadre headquarters.

"St. Yve Wood," a woman answered.

"I need to speak with Aurora Maybank."

"Lady Aurora is out for the evening."

"This is Kadenshar. I need to speak to someone regarding Destiny Rue?"

"One moment."

He was put on hold, the sounds of pianoforte filling the line. Each second felt like an hour as he eyed the girl, motionless in the bed. If a maid were to come make up the room, she'd undoubtedly conclude that the woman was dead.

"Hello?" a woman said into the line.

"Who is this?"

"Edwina, the healer."

"The girl is out of her mind, conscious but not lucid. I believe she's been terrorized by Ash Demons in her sleep."

"Why didn't you protect her?"

"I had my own battles to fight. You need to do something."

"I can't do anything from here. You're going to have to bring her around somehow."

"How in Satan's name do I do that?"

"Her core is light energy. You need to get through to that. Tell her a story, something happy, cheerful."

"I'm a demon."

"Nobody's perfect. Charter a private jet. Don't expose her to many people right now. She's extremely raw and vulnerable to their energies. If my suspicions are correct, she's been stripped of protection and exists in a cocoon of fear. You need to make her feel safe." She paused. "And loved."

Distaste filled his mouth. "That is not possible."

Silence.

"Is there anything else I can do?" he asked. Other than comfort her, make her feel warm and safe while his brother existed in a cold torture chamber?

"Crystals would help. Pick up some stones at her apartment—hematite and sodalite bead bracelets probably in her jewelry box. The hematite is dark gray or black, and sodalite is blue with streaks of white. Also, look for a labradorite wand of dark green, gray and black, and a smoky quartz point that I'm guessing would be on her nightstand."

"Smoky quartz is the stone you use to imprison us."

She ignored his comment. "Put the bracelets around her wrists. If she gets worse you will need to place the smoky quartz stone near her base chakra, facing out to draw away negative energies. It will ground her and alleviate nightmares."

And could kill me.

"She's not adept," Edwina said as if guessing his thoughts. "You say she's not even coherent."

Kade glanced at the blonde. Not conscious but still dangerous.

"Charter a plane and call me when you have arrival information. A Cadre agent will be waiting for you when you reach London. She will bring you to the castle. Don't be alarmed if Destiny stays in a coma-like state. She's terrified. Again, anything you can do to make her feel safe—"

He hung up and cursed the female he was chained to. Protect her. Make her feel safe…feel loved?

Hell's fury, he wished she were a seductress, using her powers on him in a game of wills, instead of a wounded bird needing care. Anger pumped through his mortal body, not compassion. He hadn't a clue how to express the vile emotion.

But he had to do something to get her to come around enough to walk with him, stop by her apartment and collect her things.

Of course, spending time in her apartment would make her feel safe. They would remain there, amidst the comfort of familiar things, until they boarded the plane to London.

But first he had to pull her out of her mind's solitary confinement. Sitting on the bed, he took her hand between his.

Make her feel loved.

No, he was not capable of love, yet if he could access her memories, he could discover those things that made her feel safe and cared for. He closed his eyes, drifted into a meditative state, focused on her hand sandwiched between his own…

Mother. Smiling. Holding her. Screaming. Locking her in the closet. Afraid of the dark, afraid of monsters.

Hell. Kade kept searching.

Alone on the school steps. No one to pick her up. Getting dark. Hands are cold. Nose is cold. She wants to go home. The floodlights go out, leaving her once again in the dark.

Kade had to try again…find something else…

Sitting in the lunchroom. Alone. No one notices her; no one pays attention. She is different. Strange. She'll always be alone.

An ache filled his chest.

He snapped his hands from hers. Did the girl not

have a single happy memory tucked away in her mind? If she had, it must be buried too deep for him to access. That left only one alternative—make her feel loved.

How does one love? Had his father loved his mother? He didn't know. But he did remember the way they'd touched: brief, gentle, secretive, as if they were doing something wrong.

Her rose quartz charm had settled at the bottom of her throat. The love stone. He'd read of its power after seeing it on her for the first time. But for the stone to have the most power it should be placed above the heart to heal. Could it provide the sense of love she needed to come back to him?

To him? No, back to consciousness, not to him.

Reaching out, he hesitated, preparing himself for the possibility the stone might blister his skin from being cleansed in saltwater. He clenched his jaw and touched the rose quartz. It did not burn but rather warmed his fingertips as he guided it over her heart. She moaned and turned toward him but didn't open her eyes.

Now, the hard part.

How had Father touched Mother? It was so long ago...

"You're safe, my love," he said, stroking her silken gold hair. "You are loved." The words caught in his throat. "No one will harm you now. I'm here. I'm going to protect you."

He traced his hand across her hairline and down

to frame her cheek in his palm. Stroking her skin
with his thumb, he said, "Such a beautiful creature.
Beautiful, sweet and loved."

She turned into his touch. Satan's tears! It was
working. Unfortunately, he was also getting hard.
But not for her. He didn't want *her.* Demons were
of a highly sexual nature. He needed release as a
mortal needed to breathe.

"Destiny, can you hear me, my sweet? You are
safe."

She blinked her eyes open. A hint of blue rimmed
the cold gray. They fixed on him. He slipped his
hand from her cheek and she whimpered.

"Shh," he consoled, cradling her cheek again.
"I'm here."

"I'm scared," she said in a bare whisper.

"I know."

"They are after me."

"I will protect you."

"Because you love me?"

He smiled. "Of course."

The handsome man brought Destiny to her apartment, helped her change into comfortable jeans
and a cotton shirt, then led her to the sofa and made
her tea. She felt like a princess as she watched him
gather clothes for their journey. To where?

God help her, she didn't know who he was or why
he was packing. And she was afraid to ask. What
would he do—take her straight to the psych ward?

But if he truly loved her and promised to protect her, she should be able to trust him with her secret: the fact she'd lost a part of her mind.

The last thing she remembered was dining at Salty's, the breathtaking view of the city across Puget Sound. The equally breathtaking view of her companion and his emerald-green, intense eyes, his long, wild mane pulled back and his slight smile that seemed more mischievous than pleased.

She'd been enjoying a romantic evening, remembered the way he'd touched her hand and the heat that had shot up her arm. He loved her. Warmth filled her insides. She was safe.

"It's damp this time of year in London. Do you have a favorite jacket?" he asked.

"My blue denim, in the front closet." She started to get up from the sofa, but he motioned for her to stay seated.

"I'll get it. Relax and drink your tea."

She nodded. His touch calmed her in a way she'd never felt before. She only wished she could remember more. Like how they'd first met. What it felt like to make love to him.

He suddenly turned to look at her. She blushed.

"Are you feeling better?" he asked with a smile.

"I think so." She glanced at her fingers, bare of any rings. Okay, so they weren't engaged, but that didn't mean they weren't serious.

He knelt in front of her and took her hands. "What is it, my love?"

"I…" She hesitated, then looked into his eyes. "I can't remember your name."

He blinked and forced a smile. "Kade. My name is Kade."

"How did we meet?"

"At work. It will come back to you, in time."

"Why can't I remember?"

He adjusted himself on the sofa beside her. "You suffer from a rare medical condition that causes memory loss. But it will be fine. I'm here to take care of you."

"I'm so glad." She wrapped her arms around his neck and held on. The scent of sage and spice filled her senses as she nuzzled her lover's cheek. She couldn't help but kiss his warm skin. Once. Twice. Making her way around to his mouth. God, his lips tasted heavenly.

He cleared his throat and stood.

She gripped the back of the couch to keep from melting into the cushion.

"We wouldn't want to miss our plane." He winked. "I'll finish packing."

With a smile, he went down the hall and disappeared into her bedroom.

Leaning against the sofa, she cradled her cheeks in her hands and closed her eyes. What was happening to her? She wasn't assertive with men.

This man was different. He was *the one*. She felt this deep in her heart.

She didn't have to be self-conscious around him. He loved her unconditionally.

She stood and went to the bedroom to make sure it was real, that he was real. As she hovered in the doorway, she watched him poke through her jewelry box, touching her things with a tissue. So gentle, so respectful.

"Thank you," she said.

He glanced up. "I didn't hear you come in."

"I…" What could she say? That she wanted to ogle his fine body and soak up his powerful presence? "I missed you."

"Then it's a good thing we're spending a month in England together."

"A month," she said, struggling to remember the plans they'd made.

"I've always fancied these on you." He held out dark blue and black beaded bracelets. She put them on, wanting to please him. An odd sensation tickled her hairline, as if she were remembering something about these bracelets. But it drifted away. She studied his gentle energy and protective aura.

Aura? Since when did she think in terms of auras and energies? She was a scientist who made sense of the world through experiments and equations.

"You love your stones," he said, wrapping her labradorite wand in a piece of tissue and slipping it into her denim jacket, which he held over his arm.

Labradorite. She could remember the name of the

stone but not what had happened over the past twelve or so hours.

"Now to find the quartz piece." He scanned the room. "Ah, there it is."

Again, he picked it up from the windowsill as if it were a fragile piece of crystal. Deep down she knew the pyramid-shaped stone was solid and strong. He seemed to hold his breath as he wrapped it and slipped it into a pouch in her suitcase.

"Any preference on clothing?" he asked, scrutinizing her closet.

"You choose."

"If I choose, you won't be wearing anything at all."

She blushed again. For Pete's sake, what was wrong with her? She acted like a girl on a first date with her high school crush.

"Actually, maybe you'd like to hold on to this one." He pulled the labradorite wand from her jacket pocket and handed it to her.

"Why?"

"Holding a stone seems to give you comfort."

Taking the wand, she unwrapped it from the tissue and stroked one of its polished, smooth edges. Back and forth. Her shoulder muscles relaxed, her breathing came easier. She hadn't realized the mild anxiety humming beneath the surface.

Then she glanced at Kade. She froze at the intensity of his gaze.

He wanted her. Right here, on her lace bedspread. An image flashed across her mind: Kade undressing her with his gentle, masculine hands, running his fingers down the curve of her jawline and lower, down her throat, to her breasts, brushing his palm against a rosy peak.

She automatically arched against the wall and closed her eyes. A throbbing started between her legs, and she struggled to steady her breathing, which came in short gasps.

He was touching her, wasn't he? Tracking his finger down her stomach and farther still, to caress the tender folds of femininity that ached for his touch.

"Destiny," he said.

His breath warmed her skin. He was there, skin to skin, his lips pressed against her cheek. "We cannot do this."

Yet she already was doing it. In her mind, she'd spread her legs, invited him to fill her with his love and was fondling his manhood for encouragement.

In reality, his need, hard and demanding, pressed against her jeans. His body ached with wanting. She could feel it.

"No." He grabbed her by the shoulders and broke the spell. She started to slide down the wall, but he scooped her into his arms.

She thought to place her on the bed.

Instead he carried her into the living room and set her on the couch. He stroked her cheek. "There will be a time for that. Plenty of time. Right now we need to catch a plane."

"Okay," she whispered. And couldn't wait for the "time."

Destiny awakened, disoriented and woozy, almost as if she had a hangover. Yet as a rule she didn't drink. Sitting up, she glanced out a plane window. How had she gotten here again? A headache started at the base of her neck, probably thanks to the altitude. She'd never been a very good traveler. At least she could remember that. If only she could remember the last twelve hours and how she'd met the man sitting across the aisle from her.

Kade. She sighed and studied him as he turned a page in a physics journal. She remembered watching him pack her things, going to help him, touching him…kissing…

She snapped her attention back to the window, eyeing the mass of blackness outside. Although she didn't remember how she'd met her lover, he must be a billionaire to afford traveling in this kind of style.

"How are you feeling?" he asked in that deep, rich voice.

"A headache," she admitted but didn't look at him. Every time she did she struggled not to reach out and touch him, kiss him, tear off his clothes. What the hell was that about?

"I'll get you something," he said, unbuckling his

seat belt. He stood and kissed the top of her head. "You're safe."

He disappeared into the back of the plane.

Safe? If she was out of her mind, how could she be safe?

You'll never be safe, a voice threatened.

"Who said that?" She glanced behind her. She was alone.

You are with the devil himself.

She massaged her temples. Oh, God, they were back. The voices that would drive her completely insane.

"What is it?" Kade asked, kneeling beside her and handing her a glass of water and two white pills.

"I don't fly much," she said.

The water, the way it vibrated in her drinking glass, reminded her of something. Flying, over water, without a plane.

He killed your friend.

Her friend. Adam. Adam had—

She downed the pills and handed the glass back to him.

Adam was your friend. He took care of you.

But that's not how she remembered it. She remembered the wild look in Adam's eyes as he'd pulled off her dress, his hands everywhere, his warm breath sickening against her skin.

That boy loved you.

"That wasn't love." She got to her feet, stumbling to the lavatory.

"Destiny?" Kade said.

"Bathroom." She pushed open the door, stepped inside the cramped lavatory and locked it. She had to splash water on her face to snap out of this spiral of senseless thoughts.

She glanced into the mirror. Her mother's face looked back at her. She jumped back against the opposite wall.

"Kade is not your love, Destiny," her mother said through the reflection. "He is a violent creature from the dark realm sent to trick you. They intend to sacrifice your life."

"Why?"

"Because you are a threat. You have great power."

"I don't believe you." She opened the door and slammed into Kade.

"What is it?" he asked with a hand to her shoulder.

"I need something to eat."

It had to be the low blood sugar issue, right? Then she remembered Kade's words back at her apartment: *You have a rare medical condition.*

How would he know that? How would anyone know that when her own neurologist had never given her that diagnosis?

"Is there food back here?" She fumbled through the cabinets in the galley.

"Sit down and I'll make you something." He cupped her elbow.

He'll drug your food with sleep medication, the voice taunted.

"Stop it!" She pulled away from him. "I want to make my own damn sandwich."

He eyed her and didn't let go at first. Then he nodded and went back to his seat.

That was rude, she thought.

No, it was self-defense. He is not of this world.

She leaned into the metal counter, willing the voices to stop.

He needs your powers to destroy the mortal realm.

"Damn," she muttered.

But first he will seduce you, plant his demon seed inside of you.

"Stop," she whispered.

He brought you here against your will.

No, she remembered how gentle he was with her back at the apartment.

Do you remember how he killed your friend?

"Adam," she whispered.

No one will get in his way. A demon takes what he wants. Destroys when necessary.

And his plan was to destroy her?

You must destroy him first. Use the steak knife from the second drawer as a weapon.

Blood pumped through her veins as she slid open the drawer. A serrated knife gleamed back at her.

Yes. That's the one. Grab the saltshaker.

She reached for it with her other hand.

Good girl. Stab him and throw salt in his wound. That will kill a demon. You will be safe.

She squeezed the knife handle, her fingers trembling. What was she doing? She wasn't a killer.

You will be dead by the time the plane lands if you do not defend yourself against this monster.

But if Kade had wanted her dead, he would have killed her by now. He could have killed her and left her body in her apartment. He wouldn't have gone to the trouble of putting her on a plane, flying her halfway across the world—

He lies to you. He lets you think he is your lover, but he's not. He does not care about you.

He makes me feel safe, she thought.

Lies, all lies.

"No, you're wrong," she blurted out.

God, she wanted a man like Kade to love her, cherish her. He was sexy and smart, powerful and kind.

Kind? Is kidnapping you kind?

"Destiny?" he said.

He will come up behind you, put his hand to your neck and squeeze the life out of you.

"No," she said.

Suddenly she felt a hand slide around her neck.

She struggled to breathe. Gripping the knife, her hand trembled with panic.

"Destiny, what's—"

She spun around and jerked the knife into his stomach, then tossed the open shaker of salt at him.

"Ah!" he cried out, gripping his midsection. He stumbled backward and fell to his knees.

"Destiny," he wheezed, looking up at her with watery green eyes. "Why?"

Chapter 6

He was going to die at the hand of a delusional mortal, and Tendaeus would die thanks to Kade's failure. The Grigori would get their hands on Destiny—and do what with her?

Didn't matter.

It was over.

And he hadn't even seen it coming.

The sound of roaring plane engines grew louder, pounding against his chest. He collapsed on the floor and stared up at the lights in the ceiling, then turned his head to glance outside.

Black. Like home. He wouldn't even have the pleasure of dying in his own world, where he belonged.

"Oh, my God, oh, my God, oh, my God," Destiny repeated over and over as though she were broken, stuck.

The cockpit door swung open with a bang and a familiar face loomed over him.

Pagroe. His nemesis.

"Are you all right, ma'am?" he said with a warm, soothing smile.

"I stabbed him. I didn't mean to. I thought he was going to hurt me."

"Yes, he probably would have," Pagroe said, taking her by the arm and sitting her beside Kade, who lay trembling in the aisle.

It was a slow, ugly death, to be sure.

The pain of his wound wasn't nearly as devastating as the thought of not saving his brother. He'd be responsible for yet another family member's death.

"I didn't mean to," she repeated. "He was nice to me, took care of me."

"He is an assassin for an organization in London called the Cadre," Pagroe said.

"Liar," Kade croaked, barely able to speak.

The girl's attention snapped from Pagroe to Kade and back again. "I shouldn't have stabbed him. It was wrong, but the voices—"

"Shh. He's been hired to kill you. You see, your mind challenges—" he winked "—are what make you gifted in so many other ways. The Cadre fears you and wants you dead."

Kade struggled to speak but nothing came out.

Energy drained from his body, along with the blood flowing from his stomach.

"He will be dead by the time we land," Pagroe said. "As it should be."

"Dead? No, I didn't mean to kill him."

"But you have. It's done. When we land I will take you to a lovely place in my country."

In other words, he'd lure her to the dark realm, where they'd chain her and use her for their own purpose.

He hated to think what they'd do to influence her.

"Destiny…" Her name escaped his lips. She'd be tortured and ultimately destroyed.

Because Kade was the weaker Ash Demon.

"He's lying, Destiny," Kade said.

She eyed him from her seat.

Pagroe slid his arm around her shoulders. "Here, lean against me. Do not listen to the rantings of a dying man."

"No, don't touch me." She pulled away from Pagroe and kneeled beside Kade. She touched his cheek and his skin warmed.

"It was the voices," she said, her eyes shadowed with remorse.

"Haven't you been listening to me?" Pagroe said. "This man is your enemy."

His eyelids grew heavy as he started to fade.

"This is not right," she whispered.

Kade noticed a spark of understanding in her

eyes. She didn't know who to trust, but she knew stabbing Kade had been a mistake.

"We need to help him," she said.

"The man who tried to kill you?" Pagroe countered.

"He didn't try to kill me. It was the voices— they lied."

"But he killed your friend, Adam."

She eyed Pagroe over her shoulder. "How did you know about Adam?"

"I've been hired, as well, to follow you. To protect you."

"No," Kade whispered, then coughed and rolled onto his side, gripping his midsection. At least the pain was keeping him semiconscious.

She stroked his brow. "I'm sorry. I'm so sorry."

"Stop that." Pagroe gripped her upper arm and pulled her to her feet. "There is nothing to be sorry for."

"You're hurting me." She struggled against him.

Kade's temper flooded his chest. Nothing…he could do nothing to help her.

"Let me go," she demanded.

Pagroe pulled her closer; she struggled against him.

Kade was going to die, and the last thing he'd see was Pagroe forcing himself on her.

"Damn you," Kade said.

"Damn you." Pagroe shot Kade a smile and planted a kiss on her lips. She squealed in protest, and he let her go with such force she slammed back into her seat.

Pagroe sat on the edge of his seat and leaned forward in Kadenshar's face. "She is beautiful, isn't she? And that taste? A virgin's sweetness with a heady scent, wouldn't you agree? You have tasted her, haven't you? Have you made love to her?"

Kade closed his eyes.

Pagroe slapped his cheek. "Have you?"

"No."

Pagroe's eyes widened with lust. What was it with this girl that made Ash crave her so? Kade had felt it. Yet it didn't consume him the way it had Adam and now Pagroe. Was it the lust for her power?

"Pagroe, don't," Kade said.

"You don't order me, dead demon."

Pagroe stood, straightened his tie and went to Destiny. Kade struggled to get up but only managed to lean against the armrest of a seat.

Destiny wore that lost expression again, the one where she was not quite conscious but not cataleptic. She'd be an easy victim.

Satan's tears, Kade would have to watch, helpless, berating himself for what was to happen next.

She was curled up in her chair, rubbing something in her hand. One of the stones he'd given her from the apartment. It seemed to calm her, help her focus.

"You are such a sweet, beautiful creature," Pagroe said, kneeling beside her and fingering her hair. "I will keep you safe and make you feel loved."

"Don't listen to him!" Kade spat. A demon's suggestions could easily sway a mortal, and this girl was in a fragile state.

"Shut up and die!" Pagroe stood and turned on Kade.

He kicked Kade in the gut, spearing a new round of pain throughout his limbs. Kade collapsed on the floor and felt himself drift into hallucination.

"Don't touch me," she cried.

"But I want to protect you," Pagroe said.

"You want to hurt me. Stay back."

"Come here, my love—"

"No!" she cried.

A flash of bright light blinded Kadenshar, and a thundering *bang* slammed against his chest.

A high-pitched ring surrounded him, louder, louder. The deafening sound swallowed him up.

Destiny looked at the stone in her hand, then at the empty space where her attacker had been standing.

No question—she was insane. There was no other scientific explanation.

Or had she been sucked into some kind of alternate reality?

Yeah, the reality of mental illness. Schizophrenia would explain the voices and the delusions.

She eyed the dark green-gray stone, which now glowed in her extended hand. By pointing and shouting, she'd made the delusion of the creepy guy disappear. She wondered if she could make this whole hallucination disappear.

She pointed it at Kade.

Mr. Sharpe.

She remembered now. He'd been at her lecture at Seattle University, asked her to join him in London on behalf of the ADL Trust.

They were interested in *her* research, not Professor Walingford's. She sighed, leaned against her seat and slipped the stone back into her pocket.

Mr. Sharpe had been charming, gentle and kind.

And she'd stabbed him with a steak knife. She was going to jail. *Don't kid yourself, Dee. You're going to be institutionalized. A fate worse than death.*

Death. She eyed Mr. Sharpe.

No, he had to live. She had to explain she didn't mean it, that it was the inherited mental disease that made her snap. When they landed she'd check herself into a hospital.

If they didn't take her to prison first.

"Destiny," he moaned.

She went to him and took his hand, trying to ignore the blood that darkened his shirt.

"I'm so sorry," she whispered.

"Not your...fault," he said but didn't open his eyes. "You are not...crazy." He cracked his eyes open and forced a weak smile.

A sob caught in her throat. She would not let him die. She'd had enough science classes to know where everything was and how it worked. He was bleeding, sure, but he wasn't dead. Not yet.

"Don't talk," she said. "I'm going to get some towels to stop the bleeding."

She raced into the galley, got towels and went back to him. She shoved them against his wound and noticed it wasn't that deep. The wound itself wasn't life-threatening, yet the edges seemed to be burning his skin as if the salt was acid instead of food seasoning. Could he have an allergy?

Cleanse it, something told her. Not the voices. Something that came from deep inside of her.

She used water bottles from the galley to dampen dish towels, then kneeled beside him. His breathing was erratic. She felt his pulse: it was slow and weak. He was going to lose consciousness.

"I'm going to cleanse the wound," she whispered.

He didn't respond.

She wasn't sure why, but she took off her rose quartz pendant and placed it over his heart. It had always seemed to help her.

Carefully she wiped the edges of his wound. He didn't move, yet he had to feel it.

Suddenly the cockpit door opened. "Ma'am?" a tall man wearing a captain's uniform said.

She fumbled in her pocket, whipped out the wand and pointed it at him. "What?"

Surprisingly he seemed nonplussed by the scene before him. "We're starting our descent." He eyed Kade. "You'd better buckle up."

"I'm a little busy trying to keep him from bleeding to death. Get us down—fast."

"Yes, ma'am." He shut the cockpit door. And locked it.

She continued putting pressure against his wound. The bleeding had slowed. She could use a needle and thread right about now. What was she thinking? She wasn't an M.D. She should focus on stabilizing him so they could get him to the hospital.

He stirred and the rose quartz slid off his chest. She placed it back over his heart and held it there with one hand. The stone glowed under her fingers. Great, she was about to lose her mind again. Or had she ever regained it? Wasn't this all part of the delusion?

"Destiny," he whispered.

He spoke her name as though he was desperate to tell her something, desperate for her.

You really are nuts, she thought.

"Shhh. Relax," she said. "We'll be on the ground soon and I'll get you to a hospital."

"No…hospital. You need to…" he whispered and fell unconscious.

"It's okay. It will be okay."

And it would be. Somewhere deep in her heart she knew this to be true.

Minutes later they landed and slowed to a stop. She took a deep breath and waited but wasn't sure for what. An ambulance? The men in white to take her away?

"Hey!" she called out to the cockpit.

The pilot came out of the cockpit, ignored her and released the door to the outside. Without even a "see ya" he raced down the steps.

"Get back here!" she ordered.

A minute or two passed. She assumed the pilot had called an ambulance. That's what a normal person would do.

But was anything normal about this situation?

Thundering footsteps pounded up the stairs. They were here. They would restrain her, take her away. But she had to make sure Kade was okay first.

A woman suddenly appeared in the cabin, wearing a buff coat, cut to fit a petite frame, and well-worn combat boots. A skull-fitting aviator cap, punctuated with goggles on top, covered her head of dark hair that fell across her shoulders.

Yes, Dee had certainly gone mad.

Hands to her hips, the woman eyed Mr. Sharpe, then Dee. "I'm Mersey Bane, your driver. What's all this?" She stomped over to Destiny and kneeled beside Kade. She eyed Dee's hand over Kade's heart. "Aw, that's a beauty, isn't it?"

"I'm sorry, I don't understand. He's covered in blood."

"I meant the stone. Never seen that done before."

"What?"

"The healing, of course. Rose quartz keeps the heart strong. Smart girl." She winked.

Dee's jaw dropped. What on earth was she talking about?

The girl took Kade's pulse. "Good job. I'll stitch him up and we'll get out of here."

"We should take him to the hospital."

She pulled a needle and thread from a small leather pouch at her waist. "No hospital. They'll ask questions. They wouldn't know what to do with his kind anyway. And if P-Cell gets wind of it…woo." She shook her head.

"What's P-Cell?"

She threaded the needle, hesitated and eyed Dee with round green eyes. "A group of madmen, that's what. You'd be wanting to stay away from those death merchants. At least most of them anyway," she muttered. "P-cell wouldn't hesitate to blast this handsome bloke to pieces."

"But—"

"Later. Edwina will explain it. My job is to get you back safe."

"Back where?"

"Questions, questions. Hold the wound together so I can stitch a straight line."

Dee hesitated. It would mean removing her hand from his heart.

"It's fine. His heart is strong enough now," Mersey said as if reading Dee's thoughts.

Dee removed her hand from the stone, and it faded from a warm fuscia glow to its usual milky pink color. Dee slipped the crystal back around her neck, then held the wound together while the girl stitched it. Mersey seemed more like a girl than a woman.

"Gave you trouble, did he?" Mersey asked, motioning to Kade. "They were afraid of that."

"No, actually."

Mersey looked up at Dee.

"It's my fault," Dee confessed. "I hear voices."

The girl raised an eyebrow.

"I'm crazy."

Mersey smiled, and suddenly she looked older, wiser than her twenty-some years. "You're fine."

"Of course you'd say that. You're part of my delusion."

"Really?" She turned back to finish the last few stitches. "Never been a delusion before. How do I look? Sophisticated and sexy?"

"Uh, more like something out of an Amelia-Earhart-meets-*War-of-the-Worlds* sci-fi movie."

She snickered. "You should see me on Saturdays. I look downright gorgeous."

"Why's that?"

"That's when me and my Jack go pub crawling." She winked, snipped the last stitch and packed up her things. "Ready to go?"

"I think you should drop me at a hospital," Dee said.

"What—did you get cut?" The girl ran her hand along Destiny's arm.

"No, I'm fine. I mean, I'm not fine. I'm nuts, remember?"

The girl sat back on her haunches. "Look, I know you don't know me and I look a little different than your typical American friends, but you have to trust me. You are not nuts. There's something else going on here. The Cadre will explain it to you."

"The Cadre?" Dee stood and took a step back. What had the other man said—that the Cadre had sent Kade to kill her?

"What's wrong? You look like you ate a toad."

"The Cadre wants me dead."

"What?" Mersey stood and motioned to Kade. "Did that rascal tell you that?"

"No, the other man did."

"What other man?" Mersey glanced behind Dee toward the galley.

"He was here before and now he's gone," Dee said.

"What—he jumped?"

"No." Dee pulled the labradorite wand from her pocket. "He was threatening me, so I pointed this at him and he disappeared. I'm nuts, remember?"

"Saints alive, you crystallized the bastard and you're not even an adept? I can see why they're so interested in you. Come on, we need to get back to the castle before they decide to make a ground assault."

Ground assault?

Good grief. This girl was as crazy as Dee.

Mersey grabbed Kade by his arm. "Help me get him to the Bug."

The Bug? Dee hesitated.

"Still don't trust me, do ya?" the girl said.

Dee fingered the crystal point. She didn't trust her

own mind. How could she trust this strange-looking girl with the aviator hat who wanted to take her for a ride in a bug?

"Tell you what," Mersey started. "Let's get out of here, someplace safe, and if you still want to check yourself into the hospital, I'll take you there myself. Girls' honor." She raised two fingers. Whatever that meant.

The cabin rocked with thunder.

"Bloody hell, they're close. Come on!" She gripped Kade by one arm and nodded for Dee to get the other.

"Destiny," he whispered.

"Gone soft on you, has he?" Mersey joked.

Right, he was falling for a nut job, the woman who'd tried to kill him?

"I think he's allergic to salt," Dee said.

"His kind usually is."

"His kind?"

Another rock of thunder shook the plane as Dee and Mersey awkwardly led him to the steps.

"It's going to be a big one." Mersey eyed the sky. "I figure we've got about five minutes to clear out."

They managed to get him down the metal stairs, where a white Volkswagen Beetle was waiting. Duh, of course. The model of her car.

"Get in the back with him and stay down," Mersey ordered. "If he starts to slip away, put that rose quartz over his heart."

Dee climbed into the cramped backseat of the compact car next to an unconscious Mr. Sharpe.

Mersey got behind the wheel, muttered something and tapped the dashboard. "Let's roll!"

The car sped off, faster than a little car like that should be able to drive. Dee struggled to buckle up as the girl's crazy maneuvers slammed her against Kade.

She pushed away, fearing she was hurting him.

"Bugger, coppers!" Mersey cried, then jerked the wheel left. Dee slammed into Kade again.

"If they pull me over, you stay on top of him to hide the blood," Mersey ordered.

"I don't want to hurt him."

"You won't. But the coppers will. P-Cell has spies at the Met to let them know about paranormal incidents. If they suspect anything they'll call it in to P-Cell agents for sure."

Spies. Paranormal incidents. P-Cell.

Dee's mind flooded with confusion and fear. Somehow this delusion felt very real.

She wrapped her arms around Kade and pressed her head against his chest as the Bug hit a bump, jerking them both an inch off the seat. She struggled to ignore his wound. She'd be covered with blood now, too. Blood of her own insanity.

Bright lights flashed through the windows of the little car.

"Blast, I'm going to have to stop," Mersey said. "Don't speak if you can help it. If he hears your American accent he'll want to see a passport. Stay on top of Kade. Make it seem like a romantic thing, yeah?"

Mersey slowed the car to a stop.

"Deep breaths now," Mersey coached, yet Dee could sense the girl's anxiety.

It seemed like forever before the cop approached the car. Mersey rolled down her window. "Good evening, Officer."

"Shoulda known it was you, Mersey Bane. That's it. Get out of the car. You're under arrest."

Chapter 7

Dee wasn't sure what to believe and who to trust.

But instinct told her being arrested was the absolute worst thing that could happen right now.

Lying on top of Mr. Sharpe, she contemplated her options.

Yikes. Not many, and none of them good.

She could be arrested for attempted murder and be locked away with hardened criminals; she could ask to be locked up in a mental institution; or she could somehow help Mersey out of this situation and get them both to safety.

Dee's mind had started devising a plan when the man beneath her moaned.

"Kade?" she whispered.

Nothing.

Was he dying?

"I'm going to have to ask you to step outside," the cop said.

Mersey got out of the car and chatted with the officer. Not good. Dee couldn't drive, couldn't save Kade's life.

Just as she hadn't been able to save Mom.

"No," she whispered. Her rose quartz crystal dangled from her silver chain. She remembered what Mersey had said.

Place it over his heart.

Which made no scientific sense, yet it had worked before. Okay, one thing at a time. Save the man's life, then figure a way out of this.

She wedged the charm between their bodies, above his heart.

"Kade." She stroked his pale cheeks.

She remembered how Mama used to hold her hands and they'd whisper prayers for their loved ones. Well, not prayers in the traditional sense but "star wishes," as Mama used to call them.

Then again, Mama had been nuts. But Dee had to do something for Kade, at least comfort him.

"You're going to be fine," she said. "The cop will lose interest and leave us alone. Your heart is beating stronger, you're healing."

She remembered the lyrics of a song her mother

used to sing. They had always calmed her. Dee sang softly to Kade.

"Moonlit journey,/Stars of night,/Magic wishes,/ Grace of light./See me, hold me,/Stars, they play,/ Sweet Grace, Sweet Grace,/Light the way."

Kade shifted beneath her and opened his eyes. "What… Destiny?" An incoherent expression filled his green eyes. "You're on top of me?"

"It's to hide the bloodstain on your shirt. Our driver was pulled over by the cops."

"Driver?"

"Mersey Bane."

"Pagroe?"

"He's gone."

Kade closed his eyes as if relieved.

"The cop said he's going to arrest Mersey," Dee said in a frantic whisper.

"Shh. Lay your head against my chest. Focus on my heartbeat."

"We need to help her."

"We will."

His tender green eyes touched something deep inside of her.

Trust. She trusted him. At least at this moment in time.

She pressed her cheek against his chest and took a deep breath.

"That's right," he whispered. "Focus on my heartbeat."

Dee blocked out the conversation between Mersey and the policeman.

Let the girl go.

She's got nothing of interest.

She's innocent of wrongdoing.

Dee heard the voices but didn't fear them. She breathed in and out, the echo of Kade's heartbeat vibrating against her chest.

Let the girl go.

Let Mersey Bane go.

Thump, thump, thump.

Her chest filled with light, with hope, her heart pounding in sync with Kade's.

Let Mersey Bane go.

Thump, thump, thump.

"Let her go," Dee whispered.

In her mind she drifted to a safe place surrounded by natural beauty: heather-covered fields in the distance, moss-covered trees arching across a forest trail. Tiny lights illuminated a circle in a fantastic glow.

This lightness of heart and spirit felt a lot like her experience with meditation. She floated through the vibrant enchanted forest, across the fields and up the steps of a great castle.

Safe, strong, impregnable. In this place she would be safe…whole.

The car door jerked open, jarring her out of her peace. Dee gasped, feeling as if she'd been slammed against a stone wall.

"Bloody Nora, I'm good," Mersey said, getting

behind the wheel. "Didn't think I'd be talking my way out of that one. The bloke didn't even give me a citation for driving like a lunatic."

They drove off, this time not so fast. Dee calmed her breathing.

"Must be my sparkling personality," Mersey chuckled.

"What did he say?" Dee asked as she studied Kade. His eyes were closed, his breathing shallow. What just happened? It felt like more than wishful thinking.

"He made the strangest face," Mersey explained, "like he had a sudden case of gas. Then he said, 'Mersey Bane, I'm letting you go.' And he walked away. Just like that."

Just like that?

Dee put her head against Kade's shoulder. Somehow, in this wild dream of hers, she and Kade had used their mental influence to prevent Mersey Bane from being arrested.

Not possible, not in the real world. But then, this wasn't real. It was a dream.

And in her dream she felt safe lying against Mr. Sharpe, safe in the company of the rather odd Mersey Bane who chauffeured them out of the city to the English countryside.

"Are you okay?" Kade's husky voice asked.

"You're asking if *I'm* okay? I stabbed you."

"You were frightened. Pagroe—did he hurt you?"

"Not really."

"What happened to him?"

"I don't know."

"He'll be back."

No, she didn't think so. She felt the bulge of the labradorite crystal wand against her hip bone. Vaporizing people with rocks…mortally wounding them with salt…healing them with words and crystals…it was all insanity.

Her fingers twitched as they held the rose quartz charm to his chest. Yes, that would be a trick, being able to heal without drugs or surgery. Ludicrous.

She knew it wasn't possible. No amount of love had been able to save her mother's mind—or her life. Dee had spent countless nights sitting at her window, gazing upon the stars, reciting the verse her mother had taught her. But no amount of good wishes could keep Mom from escaping the hospital and running into the path of an oncoming motorist.

Out of her mind, Dee's mom had been running from hospital personnel, the very people who could keep her safe, who could help her.

Wasn't Dee doing the same thing by leaving the country? She should have stayed in Seattle, consulted with experts at the University of Washington and sought treatment.

Instead she'd jetted off to England with a handsome stranger.

No, this wasn't real. She was probably sound asleep in her apartment, fighting off the crazies.

Oh, God, why did I have to get sick like you, Mom? I have so much left to do.

"Destiny?" Kade said.

"Yes?"

"You're not crazy."

She pushed off him and edged between the two front seats. "Yes, I am. You read my mind. That's not possible."

"I didn't read your mind, but I can guess what you're thinking. Everything that's happened in the past few hours has been rather—" he paused "—outlandish. But it's okay now. We're safe."

"If they don't try a ground assault," Mersey said.

"Stop scaring her," Kade scolded.

"Sorry, sorry."

"Destiny, lie down with me," he said. "Rest until we reach our destination."

Dee glanced at Mersey.

"It's a couple of hours," Mersey said. "Might as well."

Exhaustion flowed to every corner of her body. Dee lay against Kade and closed her eyes. Couldn't hurt to sleep. Yeah, right. Maybe if she went to sleep she'd wake up from this nightmare and be back at work or shopping at Pike Place Market.

She found herself wishing Kade would be beside her when she awakened.

Within minutes Destiny was asleep. Kade could tell by her slowed breathing and the way she nuzzled his neck. She drove him mad with desire, and in his wounded state, that was no small feat.

"What did you do to her?" Mersey accused.

"I rescued her and tried to protect her."

"No, just now. You did the mind-control thing, didn't you? You told her to sleep—and blammo!— she's asleep."

"I did no such thing."

"You'd better not try that stuff on me or I swear I'll zap ya." She waved a crystal point in her hand.

"I've heard about you, Mersey Bane. You're the paras' friend, not our enemy."

"I don't like being messed with. That mind-control stuff freaks me out."

"My dear, I couldn't control you if I wanted to. I'm worn out. My body is weak from the salt contamination. You have nothing to fear from me."

"But she does, doesn't she?"

"Not as long as she helps my brother. Have you—" He hesitated. "Do you know how he's doing?"

"He's not gone. Not yet."

Good, Tendaeus was still alive in the crystal prison.

"She's a special one," Mersey said.

Kade stroked Destiny's hair. "Yes."

"What have you heard about her?"

"That she's destined to destroy my kind with her crystal magic."

"I don't believe that. She's a healer like her mum. Healers don't destroy, they save."

"Her mother was a para?"

"That's the legend. She apparently sacrificed herself to save Destiny."

"I don't understand."

"Her mum knew instinctively of her gifts. She feared the Grigori and what they would do if they discovered that her daughter was gifted as well. So Mummy pretended to be crazy, hoping to throw them off track."

"But, in fact, she was sane?"

"Yes. To think she had to live out her life in a mental hospital, never seeing her daughter…never holding her."

"There is no insanity running through her family?"

"None."

He stroked Destiny's hair. She'd been chased by the monster of insanity all these years yet had nothing to fear.

From mental illness.

She had plenty to fear from her enemies. Was Kade still on that list?

"I thought her mother's insanity caused her to throw herself in front of a car?" Kade asked.

"No, she was running from demons who'd come to the mortal realm seeking help."

A chill raced down his spine. "Help with what?"

"I don't know the details. But she was a rumored healer, so they must have come for that."

Hell's fury. Could it be? Could Destiny's mother have been the woman his father had sought out to heal Kade's Ash illness?

Destiny's mother had caused the death of Kade's father and brother?

It made sense. His father and his brother had traveled to the mortal realm to seek help from a great healer and been turned away, then killed by P-Cell agents as they'd tried to return to the dark realm.

The vision. When he'd gone into her mind to influence her thoughts, he'd seen her mother being hit by a car and his father and his brother standing over her.

Yes, it had to be. Disgust filled his chest at the feel of her body against his. This woman's mother was the selfish mortal Kade had been cursing his entire existence.

Oh, devious fate, what fun you must be having at my expense.

His enemy lay across him, depending on him to keep her safe.

And he would until she freed his brother. It was the least she could to do make up for her mother's sins. Once Tendaeus was healed and safe, Kade would decide the next course to take. Vengeance was long overdue.

Yes, it would all come full circle. He would finally resolve his family's devastation.

Dee awakened a bit later, a little foggy and dazed. She wasn't sure how long she'd been asleep or even where they were.

"Kade?" she whispered against his ear.

He didn't answer. She propped herself up and studied his face. She placed her hand to his forehead. He wasn't feverish.

"Sleep well?" Mersey asked from the driver's seat.

"Yeah, I guess."

"Come sit up front with me."

Reluctant to leave Kade, Dee hesitated.

"He's fine," Mersey said. "Sleeping is all."

Kade shifted, as if uncomfortable, and the rose quartz crystal slid off his chest. Dee grabbed it and put the necklace around her neck. Touching his shoulder, she sensed something was wrong.

Something other than that she was going mad.

She climbed into the front seat and buckled her seat belt. "I'm worried about him."

"You've taken to him?"

She glanced over the seat at Kade.

"Blimey, he's got control over you, does he? It's a good thing we're almost there so they can talk some sense into you."

"You mean this hallucination is almost over?"

Mersey pinched Dee on the arm. Hard.

"Hey!" Dee protested.

"That's real pain. Everything that's happened to you in the past twenty-four hours has been real. It's not your mind playing tricks on you."

"I'm a scientist. There is no other explanation." Dee glanced out the window at the darkness that surrounded them.

"Did he take you flying?" Mersey asked.

Dee snapped her attention to the girl. "How did you know about that?"

"His kind likes to show off, impress the ladies."

"We both know people can't fly," Dee said.

"No, people can't." She eyed Dee. "They'll explain it at St. Yve Wood."

"Why are we going there?"

"Cadre headquarters. The Cadre was created hundreds of years ago to eliminate evil paranormal creatures and keep the world safe. The Cadre has evolved over the years. Now they're into more peaceful activities like research and development."

"What exactly do they research?"

"Paranormal activity. They hope to understand their para counterparts to better coexist."

"You mean…"

"Paras are all around us, right in front of us." Mersey winked. "Paras are not mortal. They are faeries, shape-shifters, vampires, werewolves—" she hesitated "—demons."

"Demons? As in, the devil?"

"Demons come in all shapes and sizes. They feed on our lust or greed, for instance. In some cases, with the more evolved demons, they exist to tempt us with our own ego until we self-destruct."

"What does this have to do with me?"

"Your teacher, Edwina, will explain it. Ah, here we are."

Out of nowhere a stone cottage seemed to spring up on the winding road. Covered with climbing vines and blooming pink and white flowers, the small house resembled something out of a fairy tale.

Mersey slowed the car to a stop and motioned for

Dee to open her window. As she did, she glanced up at the gates ahead. Two massive stone gargoyles guarded each post.

"Ophelia!" Mersey called. "In a bit of a rush. Have a sick one in back."

An elderly lady with beautiful skin and white hair pulled back in a bun approached the car.

"Come on, come on," Mersey muttered, glancing in the rearview.

"And who's this?" Ophelia smiled at Dee.

"Destiny Rue."

The old woman placed an open palm to her white cotton shirt. "The healer?"

"Only if I can get her safe. We really must be off to the manor. I'll stop by for tea tomorrow and we'll chat, yeah?"

"What's that in your backseat?" Ophelia made a face.

"My friend, and he needs immediate medical atten-tion," Dee said, irritated that they were wasting time.

Ophelia eyed Dee. "I see. Then continue." She glanced across her at Mersey. "Have the gargoyles check him at the door."

"Right. Great." Mersey sped away, shaking her head. "Nice lady, that one, but a bit addled. How she ever got that job…" Her voice trailed off.

"What does she do exactly?"

"She and her husband are manor guardians. There it is, up ahead."

Dee's breath caught at the sight of the castle from

her dream. The majestic stone manor was as grand as she'd pictured. Although it was nighttime, she could see it clearly up the drive. It seemed to glow with life, with magic.

Mersey pulled the car to a stop and opened her door, motioning for the footman's help. Dee hesitated, eyeing the great castle from inside the car. Mersey opened her door. "Don't be shy."

The footman helped Dee out, then reached into the car for Kade.

"Careful, he's hurt," Dee said to him.

"Welcome to St. Yve Wood."

Dee turned at the sound of the female voice. A tall, elegant woman shot Dee a restrained smile. "I'm your host, Lady Aurora Maybank."

"Nice to meet you." Dee reached out to shake her hand, but the woman ignored it and eyed Kade.

"He's hurt?"

"Yes, I stabbed him by accident," Destiny said.

Lady Aurora raised a brow and smiled. Something about the woman made Dee uncomfortable. Lady Aurora seemed haughty, slightly arrogant. And Dee was pretty sure this woman would never lose control of herself—or her mind.

The lady nodded at the girl. "Thank you, Mersey."

"It was a pleasure." She glanced at Dee. "That crystal you pointed at the man on the plane? You'd better give it to Lady Aurora for safekeeping until you learn how to use it properly."

Dee pulled the labradorite wand from her jacket. Lady Aurora wrapped it in red velvet cloth and put it in her blazer pocket.

Mersey touched Dee's arm. "I'm always around. Don't hesitate to call." She slipped a piece of paper with her phone number into Dee's hand and disappeared into the manor.

The footman was joined by a butler, who wheeled a stretcher down the steps.

"Bring him to the hospital wing," Lady Aurora ordered, distaste in her voice.

She didn't like Kade. Why? Hadn't she hired him to bring Dee to England?

The two men helped Kade onto a stretcher and carried it up the stairs. Dee followed close but hesitated when they approached the front door. Two more gargoyles bordered the entry and they freaked her out. They seemed so lifelike with their sculpted veins and vicious beaks that looked as if they could tear a man to pieces in one swift attack.

But they weren't alive, they were stone, they were harmless. With a sudden cry, their massive wings fluttered and they hovered over Kade.

"No, get away from him!" Dee cried, flailing her arms at the beasts.

Lady Aurora raised a brow. "The gargoyles must test Kadenshar's integrity," she said, as if these wild creatures attacking Kade was completely normal.

"He's in no condition for anything but medical care. Leave him alone!" Dee threw herself over

Kade's unconscious body and glared at Lady Aurora.

Kade had saved Dee's life and gotten a knife to the stomach as thanks. The least she could do was defend him against these dreadful beasts.

Lady Aurora motioned a dismissal with her hand, and they took flight, disappearing above the manor.

"Dr. Rue, your quarters are in the east wing," Lady Aurora said.

"I'm staying with him."

Lady Aurora released a sigh of impatience. "Very well."

She motioned for the men to wheel the stretcher through the front door. They walked in silence, the halls of St. Yve Manor echoing with strange sounds as apparitions floated mere inches from the high ceiling.

More delusions? What, like the gargoyles? No, they were quite real, and the sounds that echoed down the hall—chattering mixed with whispers—also sounded real.

They reached what she assumed was an examining room and the sounds quieted. She clung to Kade's arm, more out of fear than anything else. She still couldn't come to grips with the fact that her delusions were somehow real.

Glancing at a window, she noticed a collection of crystals gracing the ledge. Crystals of all shapes and sizes, from deep, rich purple to translucent yellow, grabbed her attention just as the stars had when she was a child. The crystals were fascinating, mesmerizing and quite calming. Her fear seemed to dissolve.

"Edwina will be here soon." Lady Aurora eyed Kade. "We'll finish our business later. I'll post a guard outside the door to show you to your room, Dr. Rue."

With a curt nod, Lady Aurora, the footman and the butler all left. Dee glanced at Kade and stroked his cheek. He opened his eyes, and at first she thought he was angry. Then he smiled.

"You're all right?" he asked.

"Fine. We made it to the castle."

"Good, good." His eyes drifted shut.

"Mr. Sharpe?"

He eyed her. "Mr. Sharpe? I thought we were past formalities."

"Kade." She smiled. "Mersey Bane said none of this is a hallucination, that it's real, that there's another realm, a dark realm that coexists with the mortal realm. Do you believe that's true?"

"Search your heart, Destiny. What do you believe?" he challenged.

As a scientist, these radical possibilities made no sense. Yet wasn't she also trained to keep an open mind in order to make new discoveries? She wanted to keep an open mind, she realized, smiling at Kade.

"Yes, what do you believe?"

Destiny turned at the sound of a woman's voice. Her dead mother stood in the doorway.

Chapter 8

Dee started to hyperventilate.

"Keep breathing, Dee. I'm not a delusion. I'm your aunt."

"My…aunt?" She struggled to grasp it.

"Your mother and I were adopted by two different families. You didn't know she was adopted, did you?"

Dee shook her head, clutching the rose quartz charm around her neck.

"I'm Edwina. Aunt Edwina."

She took a few steps toward Dee and extended her hand. "Don't be afraid, child. You're safe with me."

Dee shook her hand and Edwina pulled her into a loving embrace. A flood of emotions filled Dee's chest: an aunt, someone to love her and care about her. Father never had.

Her aunt broke the embrace. "Lots to digest, isn't there?"

"Yes, I'm—" She paused, considering the other-worldly creatures, her intense attraction to Kaden-shar and now reuniting with a lost relative. "Yes, lots to digest."

"We'll take it slow. I'm not only your aunt by blood but I'll be your teacher as well. I'll teach you about your special gifts, your family history and your future. You have a bright and wonderful future as a Crystal Goddess."

"What?" She stepped back and clasped Kade's hand for support. For some reason, touching him, having him close, seemed to ground her.

"I see you've made friends with Mr. Sharpe?" Edwina said.

"He protected me."

"So he has. Thank you, Mr. Sharpe, for bringing my niece to me."

He nodded. Dee sensed something more going on between them but couldn't be sure. One thing was easy to figure: no one here liked Kade.

"Destiny, I'm not sure where to start." Her aunt ambled to the other side of the stretcher and inspected Kade's wound.

"I didn't mean to do that," Dee said. "The voices…"

"Ash," she muttered. Her eyes met Kade's. He nodded.

"What's an Ash?" Dee asked.

"Later, dear. Right now, what's most important is that you're safe. Your mother went to great lengths to protect you. And now I will assume that role."

"I don't understand."

"Your mother didn't suffer from a mental disease. She feared her gift. She feared for you and what could happen if the dark forces discovered your existence. That's why she pretended to be insane, why she committed herself to a life of hell in that hospital."

"She pretended? She abandoned me on purpose?"

"It's more complicated than that."

Dee's chest ached. Her mother had been sane. They could have had years together. She could have been there when Dee won the seventh-grade science fair, when she suffered her first heartbreak.

"We have much to talk about," Edwina said. "But now we must focus on Mr. Sharpe's condition." She studied his wound. "He was stabbed, not deep, yet the wound is festering and infected."

"Salt," Kade said.

Edwina glanced from Kade's wound up to Destiny. "You threw salt at his wound? You meant to kill him? Why?"

"The voices—they said he planned to hurt me. They told me to attack him."

"Don't worry, child. They shouldn't bother you inside the manor walls. Now let's see what we can do about Mr. Sharpe's wound."

Dee gripped Kade's hand, wondering what kind

of witchcraft Edwina had planned. Dee was protective of Kade. She sensed that their connection ran deeper than the Cadre hiring him to bring her to England. He'd defended her against Adam, against Pagroe. She'd make sure he was well taken care of; she would keep him safe.

Edwina placed a few tiny green pebbles into a mortar and crushed them with a pestle.

"You're wondering what I'm doing." Edwina looked up and shot her a half smile. "Malachite ground into powder form was used in ancient Egypt to treat wounds. We'll apply it to Mr. Sharpe's wound. Help him take his shirt off."

Kade sat up and Dee carefully slipped off one shirtsleeve, then the other. When her fingers grazed his skin, he jerked as if she'd burned him.

"I'm sorry," she apologized.

"Why do you apologize?" Edwina asked.

Dee couldn't answer.

"Pay attention, Destiny. Mersey did an adequate job of closing the wound, but we need to cleanse it." She looked at Kade. "This won't be pleasant."

He clenched his jaw and stared at the ceiling.

"Destiny, hold the powder for me."

Dee took the mortar.

"Deep breaths," Edwina coached Kade.

"Do it," he ordered.

Edwina chanted something under her breath. Dee watched in rapt fascination as Edwina took the clear crystal and placed it to Kade's wound.

"Satan's tears!" he cried out, gripping the sides of the table.

Edwina glided the stone across the stitches, once, twice, then pulled it away and said, "Destiny, sprinkle the powder over the wound."

She hesitated, not wanting to cause Kade more pain.

"Hurry, child, before bacteria in the air contaminates it further."

Cupping the bowl in her right hand, Dee reached in with her left. She touched the powder and a vibration tickled her fingers. She pinched a bit between her fingers and sprinkled it over his wound.

"That's it. Very good," Edwina coached. "You're a natural."

A natural? Destiny Rue had never been a natural at anything. She'd worked her butt off for A's in school and studied cookbooks but still managed to burn toast. Trial and error. Her whole life had been one long trial.

But this treatment with rocks seemed so easy, so natural. She studied his wound. The powder eased the redness.

"Perfect," Edwina said, reaching for the bowl.

"There's more in here."

"Look at the wound, child. What do you see?"

"The skin doesn't seem as inflamed." She looked up. "How can that have happened so quickly?"

"Because of your gift, Destiny. Your touch speeds up the process. Be proud of your gift. Don't be afraid of it."

Edwina took the bowl, and Dee directed her attention, not back to the wound but to Kade's eyes. They were pinched shut.

She took his hand between her own and squeezed. "I wish I could take your pain away," she whispered and brought his fingers to her lips.

Kade was going to explode. With anger, frustration and desire. For this witch.

This witch healed you, fool. You're feeling grateful, relieved that you will live to fulfill your duty and find peace for your family.

"I'm better," he said, starting to pull away.

She wouldn't let go. The warmth from her hands flooded up his arm to his chest, surfacing to his wound, encircling it, easing the burn that the other witch inflicted with the clear stone.

Heathen's wake, Destiny was easing his pain. She didn't even understand her own strength, her own abilities.

Out of the corner of his eye he caught sight of the aunt holding something over him.

A pyramid crystal.

He rolled off the table and got behind Destiny, wrapping his arm around her neck. "Put down the crystal," he ordered.

"Kade?" Destiny questioned.

Escape. He had to get out of here, get away from the witch before she sucked him into that crystal prison.

"Clear quartz is an amplifier," Edwina said. "It will speed up the healing work we've done. If you haven't completely destroyed it."

"Kade," Destiny said, "I would never let anything happen to you. You know this is true."

And he did. Which scared the soul out of him.

The great crystal healer who could destroy his world had somehow become his protector. They'd developed a connection despite their roles as enemies. Her compassion filled his heart. He felt her there, felt the hold he had on the girl. He needed to maintain that hold if he was to save his brother.

"Please, lie back down," Destiny encouraged.

"I don't trust her." He motioned toward Edwina.

"You brought my niece to me," Edwina said. "I'm in your debt, Mr. Sharpe. My honor would not allow me to do you harm."

Destiny turned and looked into his eyes. "It's okay. Trust me."

She helped him back to the table, but he didn't release her hand. As long as he held on to her he was safe, protected. He also realized how grounded he felt in his mortal body whenever she was close.

"The quartz pyramid will be placed on the wound to speed up the work we've done there," Edwina said in explanation. "I will also place some stones to various chakra points, but you must lie still for fifteen minutes. Can you do that?"

"I'll be right here," Destiny said.

He relaxed, as if her words encased him in body

armor strong enough to repel any attack, mortal or nonmortal.

"I will lie still," he agreed.

He closed his eyes, focusing on the feel of Destiny's hand, the warmth, the vibration. He would use this girl's powers as necessary to heal and regain his strength.

He would use her powers to save his brother and seek justice for his loss.

Destiny's mother had refused to help his father and older brother years ago. She'd refused; they'd been destroyed. He would never forget this.

"Destiny, I think you should place the stones," the teacher said. "Obsidian at the base chakra to ground him…"

He felt something placed on his trousers.

"Red jasper at the sacral chakra to provide insight…" A stone was placed at his waist. "Malachite to stimulate emotional healing at the solar plexus. Rose quartz for the heart. Green kunzite for the higher heart…"

Stones were placed on his chest, one above the other, and he felt himself sink lower, lower into what felt like a mass of soft clouds.

"Amethyst to calm the mind." A stone pressed against the base of his throat. "Sodalite on the third eye for emotional balance." Another stone on his forehead. "And quartz at the crown to harmonize."

He felt pressure against the top of his head, causing him to drift, to float away.

"Destiny?"

Had he said her name? He couldn't be sure.

"I'm here. Feel my hand."

"He's not grounded," the other woman said.

Far away, she sounded far away, in another dimension. He was losing control. Couldn't move. Couldn't feel his mortal limbs.

Drifting, drifting…

"Place hematite at his feet. Quickly."

He was losing consciousness. Had it been a trick, a ploy to neutralize him by putting him in some sort of meditative state? Was it mind control?

"No," he whispered.

"Which is hematite?" Destiny asked.

"The dark, shiny stone on the tray."

"Kade," Destiny said. "Focus on my voice. Stay with me. I'm here."

Here? Where was here?

Drifting up, into the clouds.

"How's that?" Destiny said.

"Perfect," the woman answered.

An invisible force pulled Kade back from the clouds to the castle, into the great entryway, through the hallway and into the healer's room.

Close to his brother, Kade would stay at the manor and wait until his brother was released. Then they would finish what he started.

Vengeance. Closure.

They had died because of Kade, because they'd cared about him.

No, Ash did not embrace the human emotions of compassion and love.

But his father *had* loved him.

And had died for him.

Just as Destiny's mother had sacrificed her life for her daughter, compassion argued.

No, she'd been a selfish human, bent on destroying Ash Demons.

She didn't understand her healing powers any more than Destiny understands what great things she is meant for.

He didn't care. He needed her to heal his brother. He didn't care about anything that happened after that.

You do care.

No, he needed to save his brother and redeem his pathetic excuse for an existence.

Pathetic, weak son. Destroyed his family.

It was his fault.

Always his fault.

"Stop this," he whispered, but he couldn't move. Like the first time he'd awakened in the bowels of St. Yve Wood, strapped to a table, eyes covered. Here he was again, fighting for his life. They'd tricked him once more, back into their clutches. Their goal was to destroy paras of all kinds.

No, that isn't true. The Cadre isn't into destruction, P-Cell is.

"Stop," he said.

A woman said something, but he couldn't make out the words. Couldn't understand the language.

"Kade?"

Destiny's voice. He could hear her.

A woman mumbled something in the background, then Destiny spoke. "This is a normal cleansing process. Toxins are rising to the surface to be released. It's all right. It will pass."

Again he heard the other woman mutter. Then, "Ten minutes," Destiny said. "I'm holding your hand. Can you feel it?"

Feel? Touch. Destiny. Her lips. He knew what she tasted like. How could he know? Had he kissed her?

"Feel my lips on your hand," she said.

Lips. Soft, warm, loving.

Love? No. Ash did not feel love.

But his father had died because he'd loved his son. Died because of Kade.

"It's not working. We have to do something," Destiny said.

Sinking, sinking. Lower.

"Kade! Stay with me."

Pressure filled his chest.

"Open your eyes and look at me!"

He struggled to open his heavy lids and found himself looking at bright blue, like the sky on a clear day in the mortal realm. Stunning, vibrant.

"Good, keep breathing," she said. "You're going to be okay. Do you hear me?"

Blue sky all around. Could only see blue. Drifting, floating.

"Stay with me."

Pressure against his heart. Something wrapped around it, squeezing. Comforting him…

Then a woman's voice drifted down, into his chest.

"Moonlit journey,/Stars of night,/Magic wishes,/ Grace of light./See me, hold me,/Stars, they play,/ Sweet Grace, Sweet Grace,/Light the way."

Kade jerked awake with a start.

He glanced to his left. The teacher was gone, but Destiny was leaning across him, her cheek pressed against his chest. She'd interlaced her fingers with his.

How long had he been asleep? Hours? Days?

"Destiny?" he said, his voice hoarse.

"Hmm." She rubbed her cheek against his naked chest, stirring other parts of his body.

What did he expect? He was only demon.

He would not allow himself to be attracted to this girl. Closing his eyes, he took a deep breath, ignoring the warmth of her body against his. What now? He had to stay in her good graces, had to control her in order to control this situation.

Control her? She saved your life.

Whispers drifted from the doorway. He pretended to be asleep.

"How long have they been like that?" Lady Aurora asked.

"All night," Edwina answered.

"Unacceptable."

"What would you propose?"

"Destroy him."

"You made a deal. He brought Destiny to us. You owe him his brother's life. And his own."

"I don't care."

"If you break your word, you risk an assault from the entire demon population on St. Yve. All our work, hundreds of years of research would be destroyed. For what? Your ego?"

A deafening silence filled the air. He couldn't help but admire Edwina's integrity.

"The hold he has over the girl could destroy us anyway. If she's been seduced by his influence, Ash will control the balance of the universe. They are evil, hateful creatures."

"Created from human ash."

"Your point?"

"I don't think they are as hateful as you would like to believe. Things are not always defined in absolutes, Lady Aurora. There are many shades of gray between black and white. Besides, your sister fell in love with a demon and that has been a good union."

"I'm not here to argue philosophy with you. I need a progress report on Destiny."

"I'll know more once I get her alone."

"Make that happen soon. Before we lose her completely to that demon."

"Yes, ma'am."

The woman's high heels echoed down the hall.

He didn't open his eyes but felt another presence enter the room. The healer.

She sifted through things, humming softly.

Suddenly something cold and hard touched his forehead. She rubbed it against his skin in a circular motion, then traced down the bridge of his nose, over his lips and down to press against his throat. He struggled to breathe.

Not your fault.

Forgive yourself.

You were but a child.

Forgive…

He squeezed Destiny's hand and opened his eyes. He was looking up at the healer, Edwina.

"No," he croaked. "Destiny."

He felt pathetic relying on this girl to defend him.

Destiny sat up and looked into his eyes. "What? What is it?"

"My throat."

Destiny looked above him to the healer. "What are you doing?"

"Sodalite wand on the throat to help release some of his guilt."

"Destiny," he protested, barely able to breathe.

"Enough," she said. "It's not helping."

Edwina removed the stone. "I'm sorry."

And he sensed she was. Odd.

"They've set up a room for him in the east wing," Edwina said. "You'll be staying with me upstairs."

"I'll stay with Kade," Destiny said.

He took comfort that she was so protective of him.

"Why do you want to stay with him?" Edwina challenged.

"He's my friend."

"He's not your friend, Destiny. It's time you know who Mr. Sharpe really is."

"Don't you mean *what* I am?" Kade offered, regaining his voice.

Destiny looked from the teacher to Kade. "What's that supposed to mean?"

"Destiny, my sweet Destiny." His only chance was if she heard it from his lips. "I'm not capable of being anyone's friend."

"Don't say that."

"The truth is I'm not of your kind. I'm not human. I'm demon. Ash Demon."

Chapter 9

"Demon," Dee whispered. "But you don't look like a demon."

"Because I don't have horns and a pitchfork? Sorry to disappoint."

"I don't understand." Dee's mind struggled to make sense of it. Demons were evil creatures, right? Yet Kade had been anything but evil. He'd been gentle and protective. She'd read kindness in his eyes. And regret. Two very human emotions.

"He's demon. He can't be trusted with anyone's friendship," Edwina said.

"Is that what it means?" Dee challenged Kade.

"Among other things, yes."

"So you're evil?" She wanted to hear him say it. In her heart she knew it wasn't true.

Oh, get a grip, girl. You've gone from being crazy to living in some alternate universe to being in love with a demon.

"If you want to call it that, yes, I'm evil," Kade said.

Yet she read compassion in his eyes. He blinked and glanced away as if not wanting her to look too close, as if he was ashamed. He was a demon. What did it mean? She wasn't sure. But she knew in her heart that he was someone special.

To her.

"These mad scientists at St. Yve Wood blackmailed me into bringing you back in exchange for my brother's life," he said. "He is locked in one of their crystal prisons and he's dying a slow, miserable death."

She didn't want to believe that she was simply a means to an end or that he was a demon and Dee a would-be Crystal Goddess. She glanced at his wound. It had nearly healed.

Dee wanted to run, escape this place and go back to her normal, boring life. Bury herself in her research. Ignore all this.

Just like her mother?

Out of habit, she gripped her rose quartz necklace. *Listen to your heart. Let it guide you.* Instinct spoke to her.

"Why is his brother dying?" she asked Edwina.

"P-Cell agents shot him."

"P-Cell—Mersey mentioned them."

"A secret department within British Intelligence created to kill dangerous paras," Edwina added.

Dee looked at Kade. "Your brother is dangerous?"

"He's misguided. He thinks revenge will ease his pain."

"Revenge for what?"

"My father and brother were killed years ago trying to get help for me. I suffered from Ash disease as a child."

"Did they get help?"

"No, and I outgrew the disease. They needn't have sacrificed themselves for me."

The guilt in his voice resonated deep in her chest. He might be physically healed but emotionally he suffered.

And her deepest desire was to heal.

Without Kade she wouldn't have made it safely to Cadre headquarters. She would have continued to think she was mad and would have most likely been locked up.

Like Mom.

But Dee wasn't her mother. She was a determined scientist, more courageous than Adrianna Rue.

"I owe this man my life," she said to Edwina. "How can I help his brother?"

"You need to be trained in the crystal arts. You obviously have strong natural ability." She motioned to Kade's wound. "You need to sharpen it, control it. Releasing a demon from a crystal is dangerous. Demons have been—" she hesitated "—lost."

"You mean destroyed," Kade added.

"Yes," Edwina said.

"I'm not going to let that happen," Dee offered.

She squeezed his hand and he looked into her eyes. The intensity of his gaze frightened her. She read anger in his eyes, but why when she'd promised to help?

"What is it?" she confronted.

He glanced at Edwina. "Could I have a moment alone?"

"Why?" She eyed him with suspicion.

"He won't hurt me," Dee said.

"If you believe that, then he's already influenced your mind."

Edwina stuffed a small leather bag with a few polished stones and started for the door. "You need your rest, Destiny. I would recommend you finish your business with Mr. Sharpe and go to your quarters. I'll be down the hall in the library, waiting to show you to your room." She glanced at Dee and smiled. "It is good to see you."

Destiny's heart swelled. Her aunt: Mom's sister, now to be Destiny's teacher. Dee *was* special. She was extraordinary.

Edwina shut the door, leaving Dee and Kade alone. He sat up on the examining table and clenched his jaw as if fighting off pain.

"What is it?" she asked.

He glanced into her eyes. "You're not horrified by my confession of being Ash Demon?"

"I'm a scientist. We don't make snap judgments or we'd never make new discoveries. We study things to better understand them, then we make our conclusions."

"What's happened to you?"

"I'm sorry?"

"You're different from when we first met in Seattle. You're stronger, more confident."

"I guess facing death makes one stronger."

In reality, for the first time in her life she *did* feel a sense of personal power, and not because of the trauma of the last twenty-four-plus hours. Something had shifted in her psyche.

It was deeper than that. Something had shifted in her soul. Was it this place? The crystal magic surrounding her?

Or was it this man?

"I never would have let anything happen to you," he said.

"I know."

Because he cared for her? Or because he needed her to save his brother?

He tipped her chin and she looked into his eyes. When he smiled, she read more than gratitude.

She read compassion.

"You're different, aren't you?" she blurted out.

"I'm sorry?"

"Different than the rest of your kind?"

He didn't answer, but sadness tinged his deep green eyes.

"It's okay. I'm different, too," she offered. "That's why I understand you."

"Do you really? Understand me?"

"Yes, I think so."

"Then explain why I need to do this…"

He leaned forward and kissed her, his lips warm and soft, his hand gentle against the back of her neck. No man had ever kissed her like this, as if his life depended on her returning the passion.

She sensed he cared about her but fought desperately against those feelings. Parting her lips, she welcomed him, leaning into his touch. This felt dangerous, yet she ached for more. She rested her hand against his naked chest and the warmth spread up her arm to her heart.

Suddenly he broke the kiss. He pressed his forehead to hers as they both struggled to breathe as if they'd run the hundred-yard dash.

"Why did I do that?" he said.

"Doesn't matter as long as you do it again."

"Later. We both need to sleep."

Yes, she needed her strength if she was going to embark on a journey to become a crystal healer and save Kade's brother.

She leaned back and looked into his eyes. "I will do everything in my power to save him."

"I believe you." He broke eye contact. "I…I don't make a habit of believing mortals."

"Do you believe demons?"

"Not necessarily."

"Tell me about Ash Demons."

"Not now. You need to rest after spending all night working on my injuries. I—" He hesitated. "I owe you my gratitude."

Dee realized she wanted much more from this… demon.

"Let's find Edwina so she can show you to your room," he said.

"Are you going to stay at the manor?"

He shifted off the table and she helped him to the door. "Would you like me to stay?"

"Yes." She wanted—no, she needed—him near.

"Then I shall stay." They started down the hall toward the library. "I'll be close."

"Thank you. I sense you'd rather be anywhere but here at the castle."

"You're smarter than you look," he said.

"Gee, thanks. I think."

"In my experience, beautiful women have lacked in the intelligence department."

She blushed. Had he called her beautiful?

They entered the library and she spotted Edwina studying a large leather-bound book. Concern creased her features.

"Kade is going to stay at the manor," Dee announced. "I'd like him to be in a room near me."

Edwina snapped the book shut. "I'll have someone help him to his room." She pressed the intercom button by the door and requested a guard.

"A guard?" Dee questioned.

"Our guards are strong, burly sorts. Who better to help him to his room?"

"But I—"

"I'll be fine," Kade assured Dee. "You focus on yourself now, agreed?"

She looked up into his eyes. "Okay."

A tall, broad-shouldered guard in uniform came into the library. "Yes, miss?"

"Please take Mr. Sharpe to the guest quarters overlooking Mirror Pond. He'll be staying with us for a while."

The guard scowled at Kade. "Isn't he…a demon?"

"He is. And he is also Miss Destiny's guest. She's requested he be given every comfort offered to our guests at St. Yve Manor, and we will grant her request. Understood?"

Edwina's words were honest and true, although a bit stilted. She feared Kade. They all seemed to fear him.

Dee would have to research Ash Demons to figure out what was so terrifying about them.

"Yes, miss." The guard went to Kade and offered his shoulder for support. "This way—" he hesitated "—sir."

"Wait," Dee said. She got up on tiptoe and kissed his cheek. "We'll talk tomorrow."

"Sleep well."

She sensed he wanted to say something else, but he didn't.

"You, too." She smiled and watched as the guard led him out of the library.

Dee cradled her cheeks with her hands. Her whole life had been jerked sideways. She wanted some balance.

"Destiny?" Edwina came up beside her. "How are you, dear?"

"I'm scared," she blurted out.

"Of what?"

She looked into her aunt's eyes. "I'm scared of you, this place…my own—" she cleared her throat "—gifts."

"Fear will only bring nightmares and block your development. I can show you how to work with the crystals to dissolve that fear."

"What if I can't help him? What if I can't save his brother?"

"Shhh." Edwina placed a hand on her shoulder. "You're overwhelmed right now. You need to rest."

No, she needed Kade. Beside her, holding her hand, protecting her. God, how had she become so dependent on this stranger…this demon?

Where was he?

Kade surfaced to consciousness but was unable to move, unable to form thoughts. The last thing he remembered was being led out of the library, away from Destiny.

Then nothing.

Had he somehow made it back to the dark realm?

No, he wouldn't have left his brother at Cadre head-quarters. He struggled to open his eyes against the brightness that blinded him. Where the hell was he?

"Is he awake?" a woman asked.

Not Destiny. Lady Aurora.

"Not yet," Edwina answered.

He must have slept all night. He couldn't remember.

"When he wakes up, finish it," Lady Aurora ordered. "Do whatever is necessary."

"But, Lady Aurora—"

"You dare argue with me? Has the demon influenced you as well?"

"No, but I'm not sure it's wise to destroy the one person that Destiny trusts."

Destroy? Demon's curse, they were going to kill him. Why? He'd done what they'd asked, brought the girl back safe and unharmed.

He should have expected as much. Mortals were manipulative, power-hungry creatures.

"The fact that she is attached to this demon is all the more reason to destroy him," Lady Aurora said.

Kade struggled to breathe, to focus on talking his way out of this.

"Did you ever consider that breaking her attach-ment to the demon could mortally harm her?"

"What are you talking about?" Lady Aurora said. "His kind don't tap mortals to cross over."

"I sensed something during his healing process. A powerful energy between them."

"He left his demon essence inside of her?" Lady Aurora said, horrified.

"Something else, a stronger connection, almost like…"

"What?"

"I can't say for sure, but instinct tells me that destroying this Ash could cause irreparable damage to Destiny."

"Ridiculous. The feelings would have to be mutual. Demons are incapable of love."

"But your sister's demon, Galen—"

"Enough."

A few minutes of silence passed.

Kade lay there, immobile, realizing they had once again strapped him down, but this time, instead of covering his eyes, they shined a painfully bright light in his face. Why—as an interrogation technique?

"Crystallize him," Lady Aurora ordered.

Kade's pulse quickened, his palms sweated. Humanlike symptoms of fear spiked an adrenaline rush.

No, he could not be imprisoned. He needed to free his brother, take him back to the dark realm, where they could live out their days in peace, taunting mortals every now and then but not causing any real trouble.

He'd even thought he might mate with a female demon and create offspring of his own.

"No," Edwina said. "I am a healer, not a killer."

"Then use your crystals and find out what he's up

to. Dig into his psyche. Infuse him with compassion until he begs for mercy."

"You're asking me to torture him?"

"I'm ordering you to do your job."

"The crystals are used for healing, not destruction."

"Fine. Guard! Bring Mersey Bane down here. She'll crystallize him. A few days in a crystal and he'll be begging to confess all his sins."

"Stop, Lady Aurora. Don't. Let me—" She hesitated. "Let me try something first."

Hell, no. What was she going to try—white magic to torture him further? Strip his mind of his identity, his mission?

He would be eradicated here, in the basement of the castle, unable to regain his family's honor, save his brother, save himself.

He wanted to cry out, but his human vocal cords were twisted and pinched. What good would it do? No one could hear him. No one could help him.

Except…

Destiny. Help me.

"Hand me my stones," Edwina ordered.

Don't let them destroy me.

"I've heard about this radical method of cleansing," Edwina said.

A cool stone was placed on his naked chest, another on his throat.

"It's a releasing exercise meant to bring buried secrets to the surface."

"A sort of truth serum?" Lady Aurora asked.

"Yes."

A cool, smooth stone rubbed against his forehead, up and down, up and down. Edwina chanted a verse in a soft whisper. Running the stone up and down.

Up and down.

He was floating, helpless, terrified.

Destiny, don't let me go. Find me. Help me.

Suddenly a sharp point pressed against his forehead and his mortal body was pulled apart, opening his chest.

"No," he groaned.

Destiny, find me.

Bright images flashed before him: the concern creasing his mother's brow; his father kissing her, nodding at Kade.

His father's bloodied mortal body lying in pieces on the ground, P-cell agents standing over him.

Smiling.

Laughing.

Louder.

Destiny, save me.

Another image flooded his thoughts: a woman lying on the ground with limbs folded backward, blond hair covering her bloodied face. A child kneeled beside her, shaking her shoulder.

Mommy? Wake up, Mommy.

The girl was Destiny. Grief consumed him, hitting him in the chest like a ten-ton wrecking ball.

I need my mommy, she wailed.

The sound…her pain…felt like a hundred nails shooting from a blaster, hitting Kade in the chest and arms, penetrating his entire body.

Her pain suffocated him. Couldn't breathe.

Pain from losing her mother.

Because Kade's father had chased her into the street.

His fault. His father's death, his brother's death. Her mother's death.

"What do you want?" He gasped for air, his cheeks burning.

"What are your intentions?" a voice demanded.

"To save…my brother."

"What else?"

"Nothing else. For Satan's sake, release me!"

"Not until you tell us about the Grigori's plans."

"I do not know."

Destiny, I need you.

"Crystallize him!"

"Destiny," he whispered.

Her name would be his last utterance.

"What are you waiting for? Mersey, I order you to crystallize him."

"But, Lady Aurora…"

Let go, relax, don't fight it. It would only be more painful if he fought it.

"What the hell is going on here?"

Destiny. She'd come.

"What are you doing to him?" she demanded.

Whoosh!

The pain against his forehead and his chest snapped free, as if iron claws had released their hold on his heart. His chest closed up, burying his secrets, his guilt.

"How did you find this room?" Lady Aurora said.

"Like it matters? You were torturing him!"

She stroked Kade's forehead. He started to come back down, breathe normally.

"He's a demon," Lady Aurora said.

"And I'm going to be a crystal healer. And Mersey's a demon hunter. And last time I checked, Edwina, you were a healer as well. So? We're all different, not quite mortal. What were you doing to him, Edwina?"

"Releasing old memories."

"More like torturing him. What the hell is with you people? You send him across the world to find me and bring me back. I could have been killed, but he saved my life more than once. And this is how you thank him?"

She released his wrist from the binding and in a soothing gesture she rubbed his hand, then interlaced his fingers in hers. His heart regained its normal pace. He was safe. He was with Destiny.

"This demon has too much influence over you," Lady Aurora said.

"Is that what you think, Edwina?"

Silence. Then, "No, I don't sense that."

"But you still tortured him?"

"I did not hurt him. I released negative—"

"Didn't hurt him? Look at this man. In this form he's a mortal man. Mortal and vulnerable, like you and me, with a flawed and fragile physical body and a fragile mind. How could you? You're no better than the demons that torture humans."

A hush filled the room. Kade gained strength from the feel of her palm against his. The warmth melted the terror from his mind and grounded him.

"You say you're about study and healing, about peace and understanding," Destiny said. "Is it all a lie?"

This woman did not sound like the girl he'd watched stumble over her words at Seattle University. She sounded like a warrior, a leader.

"Kade saved my life. I want him to be safe. I'm going to help him find his way back to his world."

"Destiny, no," Edwina hushed.

"Don't be a fool," Lady Aurora said.

"I believe in what's right and just. It's right to give this man his freedom. Come on," she said to him. "Let's get you outside."

"Outside?" Mersey questioned.

"Something tells me if I get him to the forest, he'll be safe."

"Ash Demons are playing mind tricks on you, drawing you close so they can attack," Lady Aurora said.

"Does he look in any condition to play mind tricks?" Dee challenged.

Lady Aurora didn't answer.

"Kade, let's go."

Destiny helped him off the table. His legs felt weak.

"Arm around my shoulders," she coached.

Touching her, making that connection, seemed to strengthen him somehow.

They walked past Lady Aurora, who looked down her nose at them, then past the quirky Mersey Bane, who'd been ordered to crystallize him yet refused the order. Regret colored her eyes.

Destiny hesitated as she passed Edwina. "And you're my teacher?" Destiny said in a shaming tone. The woman studied her hands, folded in front of her.

With each step up the stairs, away from them, he felt his strength flow back into his mortal body. But his mind was still fuzzy. Would he be able to find his way to the portal in this condition?

"You're feeling better." She said it like a statement.

"Yes. How did you find me?"

She glanced up and smiled.

"You heard me?" he asked.

"Not exactly. I felt, in a word, terrorized. For some reason I knew if I found the basement holding chamber, I could stop the images from consuming me."

"You felt what I was feeling?"

"I think so." She led him to the front door.

"I'm sorry."

"You shouldn't be apologizing. Let's get you back to your world."

"I'm not sure I have the strength to find my passage."

"I'm here. I'll help."

"I shouldn't leave my brother." He glanced over his shoulder as they closed the door behind them.

"You can't do anything for him now, and being here is too dangerous."

She led him down the front steps and across the grounds, toward the forest.

"Destiny, you should go back," he said. "It's not safe for you in the woods. There are all kinds of threatening creatures."

"I've heard the stories. I'm not afraid."

And he'd heard stories of a great Crystal Goddess wanting to destroy his kind. This woman, holding him up, helping him find his way, was not a destructive force.

In the distance he spotted a soft glow of orange, red and gold. The traiectus.

"It's there." He pointed.

"I can't see it."

"It only appears to Ash Demons."

As they got closer, the portal lights dimmed. They were but fifty yards away when a strong wind pushed against his chest and whipped her blond hair about her face.

"Storm's coming," she said.

No, not a storm. Ash Demon: an entire clan, coming for her.

"We need to go back," he said.

"What? Why?"

"Our hero Kadenshar," a deep voice boomed. A crack of black lightning punctured the earth and they were tossed twenty feet onto their backs.

"Kade?" she said, out of breath.

"Kadenshar, the hero of the Ash. He has brought us the Crystal Goddess so that we might destroy her."

Chapter 10

The look of horror in her eyes stabbed Kade's heart. Did she really think he'd planned this?

"Destiny, listen to me," he whispered. "There is only once chance to survive. You must trust me. Completely."

She glanced over his shoulder. With a gentle touch, he guided her gaze back to his. Fear sparked in her bright blue eyes.

"They can only hurt you if you make yourself vulnerable." He leaned close and kissed her cheek, then whispered in her ear. "Follow my lead and all will be well."

"Kadenshar!" a voice called. "Bring us the girl."

"Pretend you are under my control," he whispered. "Like you've been hypnotized."

She closed her eyes and he straightened to address the demons. They'd sent a dozen men to retrieve the girl. They wore black uniforms but carried no weapons. No traditional weapons, anyway.

"Who is in charge?" he asked.

A soldier stepped forward.

Kade recognized Pagroe's brother. Ah, another bargaining chip. He'd overheard Mersey mention that Destiny had crystallized Pagroe.

"This is premature," he said. "The girl has not reached her full potential. As a mortal she is useless to us."

Pagroe's brother started toward Destiny. "They want her destroyed."

"They? Surely you don't mean the Grigori."

Pagroe's brother narrowed his eyes at Kade. "You've spoken with them?"

"I have. Destroying the girl was not the order. They want to control her powers."

"Then we will take her back."

"If you do this, you risk your brother's life."

Pagroe's brother stopped short of Destiny and frowned at Kade. "What do you know of my brother?"

"The Cadre has imprisoned him in a crystal."

"Savage saints," he swore.

"Once Destiny reaches her potential she will have the power to release Pagroe to the dark realm.

Allow her to go free and she will be indebted to you."

Pagroe's brother studied Destiny. She lay still, but Kade sensed her panic.

Easy, lovely. I will not let anyone or anything harm you.

"I must take her back," Pagroe's brother said. "The Grigori—"

"Will discipline you for your carelessness," Kade said.

Pagroe's brother glanced at Kade.

"She is not ready," Kade explained. "She would be of no use to them now."

"Protecting our kind from this creature will be very useful," he argued.

"Influencing her will earn you more respect. I'm developing that influence."

"Show me." He stepped back.

"Destiny," Kade said, hoping she'd follow his lead. "Stand up."

She opened her eyes and got to her feet, staring straight ahead as if in a trance. Excellent.

"Do you want to please me?" he said.

"Yes, my master."

"Then come here and show me how you please a demon."

She didn't move at first.

Touch me, Destiny. Run your hands across my chest and kiss me. Act as if you love me.

Love? Of course, that's how mortals understood

passion. It wasn't simply the need to satisfy sexual desires. For mortal women, sex had to come with love and compassion.

Dreadful, unyielding chains of emotion.

Destiny came toward him and spread her hands across his chest, studying it with such wonder. Her fingers fanned out, sliding across his shoulders. When her lips pressed against his nipple, he clenched his jaw, fighting off his body's natural response. Heat seared through his skin, past his rib cage, filling his chest. What was happening to him?

"Are you sure she doesn't have influence over you, Kadenshar?" Pagroe's brother mocked. A few of his demon soldiers chuckled behind him.

"I will never allow a female, be it Ash Demon or mortal, to have that kind of power."

Pagroe's brother shook his head. "I will take her now."

He reached for her arm, but Kade grabbed the demon's wrist and pulled him close. "Let me finish my work. Three days and she will be completely under my power. I will command her to free Pagroe. You will have your brother and the Grigori will have control over the powerful Crystal Goddess. You will be rewarded for saving the Ash Demon race."

"Three days?"

"Yes."

Pagroe's brother reached out and touched her hair. She didn't flinch, didn't stop her nuzzling and kissing of Kade's chest.

"You will bring her here, to the traiectus?"

"I will."

"I have your word, Kadenshar?"

"You do."

"Very well." He took a step back. "Be sure you don't fall under her spell and end up in a crystal prison along with our brothers."

"That won't happen."

"I will report on your progress to the Grigori."

Destiny continued to kiss his chest. He grew stiff with need. Pagroe's brother glanced at Kade's breeches.

"Enjoy yourself." He motioned for his men to follow him into the traiectus.

With a burst of light, they disappeared, the fiery circle evaporating into mist.

"They're gone," he said.

But she didn't stop her tender caresses, stroking his chest, layering wet kisses across his skin.

"Destiny, you can stop," he choked through growing desire.

Instead she pressed kisses down the center of his chest…lower…lower, brushing her lips against his stomach, her fingers unbuttoning his black slacks as she knelt on the ground before him.

Sweet demon, what was she doing to him?

Was Pagroe's brother right? Was Kade in danger of losing his will to the influence of this enchanting creature?

"Destiny," he hushed, trying to focus. Had to focus.

This fondling, this foreplay, could only lead to mating, which would lead to what? The loss of her powers? No, she would have to mate with a man she loved in order to lose her powers. Yet they did not share love.

"Destiny, stop." He gripped her shoulders and pulled her to her feet.

The hollow look in her eyes shot panic to his core. Her normally blue eyes had grown dark, almost purple, and although she looked at him, she didn't seem to focus. What was this? Had the Ash Demon soldier cast a spell on her? A spell so she couldn't resist an Ash?

Which meant she'd be vulnerable to them at any time.

"Wake up!" he ordered with a firm shake of her shoulders.

"Make love to me," she demanded.

She licked her bottom lip, slowly, with purpose, and he thought he'd go mad.

He was tempted, sure. But if he mated with this goddess, he wanted it to be on his terms, because she begged him for it. Not because she'd been manipulated by a dark spell.

"Please, Kade," she whimpered. "Make love to me. Right here, in the forest, right now!"

This was not her own will speaking. He needed to break the spell. He eyed St. Yve Manor in the distance. If he returned, they would probably torture him again, hammer him with their magic to drive him insane.

"Make love to me! I need Ash seed in my body!" She broke free of his grip and started in the direction of the traiectus. "I need Ash. I need Ash."

"Destiny, no!" His body still weak, he loped after her and grabbed her arm. "Stay with me."

"I'm going to die unless you make love to me." She fell to her knees and sobbed.

He hadn't a clue how to break this spell, but making love to her wouldn't do it. He suspected Ash had given her a suggestion that would make her want more once she got a taste of it.

They had infected her with an addiction for Ash Demon.

He needed help. "Destiny, my love," he started, kneeling in front of her. "I will make love to you. All night, I promise. But not here, not where we're most vulnerable. Come back to the manor with me. I will show you how an Ash Demon makes love to a woman, for hours, for days, without rest."

She looked into his eyes and blinked. "Days?"

"Yes."

She stood, interlaced her arm in his and practically skipped toward the manor. His only hope was that the teacher, Edwina, had some form of elixir for this spell.

"Days and days and days," she whispered.

He clenched his jaw. To think they'd poisoned her so easily, so quickly, and he hadn't even noticed. What the devil was the matter with him?

He was weak, worn down by the mental torture of the Cadre.

"I can't wait, I can't wait!" she said.

They started up the stairs and the door opened. Edwina and Mersey Bane greeted them with quizzical expressions.

"Out of our way," Destiny demanded. "I need to mate with this Ash!"

"Get your guards to restrain her!" he ordered Edwina.

She hesitated.

"Now!"

She spoke into an intercom system as Destiny pulled Kade toward the stairs.

"She's been poisoned with demon lust. The Ash soldiers in the woods planted a suggestion in her mind and I can't break it. You have to do something," he said to Edwina.

"What kind of spell?" She followed them up the stairs.

"Demon seed, I need demon seed in my body!" Destiny howled.

"I'm not sure," he said. "They didn't speak it. Probably a mating spell."

"Thank God she's wearing the bracelets or it could have been much worse," Edwina said.

They reached the top of the stairs and Destiny started down the hall. "I need to mate with this Ash!" She tried a bedroom door. Locked.

"Where are your guards?" he demanded.

"They're coming."

Edwina followed them to the next room,

studying Destiny's eyes, the flushed color of her cheeks, probably trying to determine how to treat the condition.

Kade heard guards storm up the stairs. Destiny reached a third bedroom and flung open the door.

"Make love! Make love to me, Ash!" she ordered.

"Guards, in here!" Edwina called.

They raced into the bedroom and grabbed Kade.

"Not him. Her!" Edwina said.

Destiny flopped on the canopy bed and stretched out her arms and legs as if waiting for him to take her. He gripped the bedpost for support, fighting his most basic need to mate with the blond beauty.

The guards pulled her off the bed.

"Take her to my room and restrain her so I can examine her," Edwina said.

"No, no!" She fought. "Kade, help me!" she cried. "You're supposed to protect me! Make love to me! You promised! How could you lie to me?"

Each cry felt like a knife to his chest. Why? He hated these feelings, despised that mortal part of him that allowed him to feel regret or remorse.

"Kadenshar! You promised! Mate with Ash, need to mate with Ash…" Her voice echoed down the hall.

He sat on the bed, blinking back his rage at his fellow Ash. They had turned an innocent, magical girl into a creature of lust.

"I am in your debt."

He glanced up. Edwina stood in the doorway.

"You owe me nothing. I have selfish motivations. You know that."

"Do I?" She hesitated as if waiting for him to elaborate, confess his true feelings.

Which were? He hadn't a clue.

"Thank you." Edwina left to tend to Destiny.

Now what? It's not as though he could return to the dark realm for sanctuary. He'd promised to stay with her, influence her and deliver her to Pagroe's brother three days from now. He couldn't return to his own world without her. They'd know he'd lied, broken his word to present the girl.

Pagroe and his brother seemed to be liars as well. First Pagroe pretending to be Kade's friend, beating him at the Grigori council, then trying to seduce Destiny on the plane. Pagroe had no doubt driven her to stab Kade, practically killing him with the salt infection.

And now the brother had planted a seed of lust in her mind, knowing it would make Kadenshar's job more difficult. So much distrust among his own kind, between the mortals and the paras.

Destiny had trusted him, trusted his word when he'd promised to make love to her.

No, that was not Destiny. That was the shadow side of her, poisoned by Ash Demon.

"You've risked your life coming back here."

He glanced up at Mersey Bane, who stood in the doorway.

"Are you going to crystallize me?" he said.

"No." She leaned against the doorjamb and crossed her arms over her chest. "I'm going to invite you to stay at the manor for a while."

"Not a good idea."

"Lady Aurora has gone to London. She won't be back for a week. It's safe."

"I don't belong here."

"Where do you belong?"

He wasn't sure anymore.

Thundering footsteps echoed down the hall. An out-of-breath guard raced to the room. "The healer needs you."

He started for Kade. Mersey placed a hand on his arm. "Stop. You don't need to treat him like the enemy. He'll help on his own."

Kade managed to get to the stairs, gripped the railing and started down. Damn, his brain was infected with weakness if he thought these people wouldn't kill him at their first opportunity. If he stayed, he surely would be crystallized.

He eyed the front door, wondering if he should whip it open and fly his way to freedom.

"Kadenshar! Help me!" Destiny's pleas carried down the hall.

The panicked edge of her voice drove him to the healing room. He froze in the doorway as he watched three guards struggle to hold her down.

Their hands were all over her.

"Don't touch her!" he demanded, going to her side.

One of the guards blocked him.

"Away!" Kade flung his arm and the guard floated away from the table. How could that be? In his weakened state he shouldn't be able to move objects.

The other two willingly stepped away from the table.

He took Destiny's hand, squeezed it and looked into her eyes. "Look at me, lovely. You're fine. Everything's fine."

"Keep her calm so I can perform this ritual," Edwina said.

"Kadenshar, mate with me! Do it now!" Destiny cried, writhing, trying to escape.

Edwina bound her around the waist, ankles and wrists.

"She's too excited," Edwina said, lighting a sage stick, another instrument of mortal cleansing that could burn a demon's lungs.

"Should I put it out?" Edwina must have sensed his worry.

"Not if it will help."

"Mate with me, fill me with your seed!" Destiny demanded.

"Destiny, love, I can't mate with you if you're worked up like this. You need to calm yourself."

"Tell me how you're going to make love to me. Tell me."

"Shh. If you calm yourself, I will tell you." He paused. "In great detail."

"Okay, okay. Calm, I'll be calm." She closed her eyes. "Tell me."

"After a romantic dinner, I will carry you to your room and place you on the soft bed."

He nodded to Edwina. She started her chant in a low, monotone voice.

"Measured trail…gift of light…release this girl… sweet moon's delight…"

"Slowly, with great precision, I will unbutton your blouse," he continued. "I will spread it wide so I can take in the beauty of your skin, your perfect breasts."

"My bra, take off my bra."

"Shh. In good time, my love."

"Measured moon…secrets told…break the chain…release the hold…"

"I will run my hands along your sweet, firm calves, naked beneath the skirt you wear, then I will part your legs and trail my fingertips up to the soft nest of curls needing to be touched."

Destiny writhed against her bindings and arched her back as if she felt his hands touching her, caressing her.

"With my fingers I will stroke the tender mound of desire until you beg for release."

He clenched his jaw. His own desire was starting to stir, damn it.

"Sunstone reins…I place this stone…near her heart…release her chains."

Edwina placed an orange-yellow stone on Destiny's forehead.

"Kadenshar?"

Afraid she'd move her head, he placed his hand to her cheek and spoke very close. She pinched her eyes shut.

"I will remove your skirt and panties, sliding them down and off your legs. Then I will unhook your bra and cradle the warmth of your breasts in my hands."

The sage, it was making him light-headed.

"*Ooommmmaaaatttaaa...ooommmmaaaatttaa,*" Edwina chanted.

"I will taste you with my tongue. First your breasts... I will lick your nipples, sucking one between my lips and biting down ever so gently."

Heaviness settled in his chest and climbed up his throat.

"Can you feel it, my sweet? Feel the pinch of my mouth over your breast?"

"More..." she whispered.

"Then the other... I will nuzzle and kiss my way to the other breast, but this time I will be trailing my fingers down your fair, sweet skin to the soft mound that aches to be touched."

Edwina's chant grew louder, more persistent.

"Touch me," Destiny whispered. "Touch me there."

"I edge my finger between your feminine folds and..." He was going to pass out. No, had to keep at this, had to make her better.

"You welcome me, beg me to enter you, fill you with my power."

"Kadenshar…Kadenshar," she moaned.

"I climb on top of you. Your pussy throbs with anticipation, aching for my heat."

Edwina's voice hit a crescendo. *"Liberatio!"*

"Kadenshar!" Destiny cried, arching her back.

Kade collapsed to the floor, struggling to breathe. The sage must have poisoned his lungs. His body spent, he sat limp on the floor. He glanced at Edwina, who leaned against a metal cabinet, gasping for breath. The guards had collapsed to the floor. Destiny had passed out, a content smile creasing her lips.

Edwina looked at Kade. "What was…that?"

"You want the technical term?"

Edwina blushed. "Oh, my God."

"Demon, actually."

Chapter 11

The next morning Dee awakened in an incredibly soft bed feeling completely sated, as if every part of her body had stretched out its kinks and had been rubbed smooth.

She sat up in bed with a start.

Rubbed?

Touched?

Stroked?

Yowsa! She'd had an orgasm at the hands of…Kade? A demon?

No, something wasn't right. The last thing she remembered was helping him outside to the forest…the Ash Demon soldiers coming…being terrified that he'd tricked her, that he was turning her over to the demon clan.

No, he was going to protect her.

But she had to fondle him, kiss him and…

Sex. They'd had sex? Maybe. Kind of. Not really.

"What is happening to me?" She cradled her head in her hands.

Someone knocked on her door. Although dressed in flannel pajamas, she pulled the covers to her chin. "Yes?" It sounded more like a squeak than an invitation. Could it be…

…her lover?

Edwina pushed open the door. "Good morning, sleepy girl. How are you feeling today?"

"Today? What day is it? How long have I been out?"

"A full twenty-four hours." Edwina went to the armoire and pulled out a pair of leggings and a lavender cotton tunic. She brought them to the bed. "We were worried about you."

"What happened?"

"You don't remember?"

"I remember taking Kade into the forest to protect him from you people."

"He has nothing to fear from me, Destiny. He saved your life yet again. He is not what we first thought." She hesitated. "Although he is still demon and he can't be completely trusted. But he feels more compassion than most of his kind."

"He saved me again? From what?"

"Ash Demons wanted to take you back. He talked them out of it, but they cast a powerful lust spell on you. He helped me release you from the spell."

"Oh." She couldn't keep the disappointment from her voice. She'd actually hoped her dream of Kade making love to her had been real.

"What is it?" Edwina asked.

"Nothing. Did he leave?"

"He would prefer to stay at the manor until we're able to release his brother. Unless you'd rather he go."

"No," she said anxiously—and caught herself. "No, he can stay. What about Lady Aurora?"

"Gone to London. He's safe." She touched Dee's shoulder. "You're safe as well. I'm very sorry I upset you yesterday when I was working on Kadenshar. I hadn't meant to hurt him, but apparently his memories, his guilt, is very painful when it's brought to the surface for release."

"But Lady Aurora—"

"Wanted to crystallize him, I know. I was trying to offer an alternative, a way to prove he is our friend, not our enemy, in the hopes she would abandon that notion. She abhors demons. One tried to rape her when she was seventeen. I'm afraid she's never fully recovered from the trauma."

Dee could understand the feeling. Adam had tried to force himself on her only days ago.

"We have much to talk about," Edwina said. "It's imperative we start your training as soon as possible."

"So I can save Kade's brother?"

"That's one reason. Destiny, the dark forces don't understand you, they fear you. Once you achieve your highest potential, you will not be vulnerable to them. You can prove that you are not to be feared but rather respected, that you have no plans to destroy them. But until you've reached your goddess status, you are in danger. They will do everything in their power to hurt you."

"You mean destroy me?"

"I won't let that happen. Neither will Kadenshar."

"He needs me to live so I can free his brother."

"Yes."

"Why can't anyone else free his brother?" A part of her wished Kadenshar wanted Dee for who she was, not for her healing ability.

Edwina shifted onto the bed. "His brother is injured—mortal injuries, but they are suspended in the crystal. When released, oxygen will hit his wounds and make them worse. We need to heal him inside the crystal."

"Have you done this before?"

"No."

"Then why do you think I can do it?"

"Because you're the light-haired, blue-eyed beauty of legend. The Crystal Goddess, the daughter of a twin healer."

Dee hesitated before asking the next question. "What was she like?"

"Your mom?"

Dee nodded.

"She was a wonderful woman, bright and crea-tive. She loved you." Edwina smiled.

"Not enough to hang around."

"Don't you do that." Edwina stood and placed the clothes on the bed. "I never want to hear you feel sorry for yourself. Your mother loved you so much she pretended to be crazy. Do you have any idea what it was like to live locked up with mentally ill people for nearly ten years?"

Dee shook her head in shame.

"It was horrible. I visited once. She told me never to come back. She told me not to seek you out, that I would be putting you in danger. I em-braced my gift of healing. She feared it. What will you do?"

Dee had lived her entire life in fear of going crazy and was damn tired of it. Yet to embrace her new abilities Dee would have to turn her back on her career as a scientist, a career she'd chosen because she wanted to heal people. Isn't that what she was doing in her newfound role?

"I'd like to learn more," she said.

"Excellent."

"And help Kade," she added.

"Okay, then get dressed and meet me downstairs for breakfast. You should be fully nourished before we get started." Her aunt went to the door.

"Edwina?"

"Yes?"

"I know I shouldn't feel sorry for myself. I just wish I would have had more time with her."

"Me, too, sweetheart. Me, too." Edwina shut the door.

Dee stretched and got out of bed. She ambled to the tall leaded-glass windows and glanced outside. A slight mist was rising from the lush green lawns.

Green like Kade's eyes. Green, calming, gentle. What was it about this…man…demon…that made her feel safe and whole? And why didn't she mention that bit of information to Edwina? Did she fear her aunt would order Dee to stay away from him? They all seemed to fear Kadenshar as much as the Ash Demons feared Dee.

So much fear and distrust.

Things were much simpler in her career as a scientist. She could make sense of the world and explain away mysteries.

She wished she could explain the mystery of why she trusted Kade so much, maybe even more than she trusted her aunt. Glancing out the window, she marveled at the forest on the perimeter of St. Yve. It was enchanting and maybe a bit seductive. Something tugged at her heart, pulling her there.

Dee stepped back from the window. Was it light energy or dark? Ash Demon forces?

She had a feeling that the sooner she developed her healing powers, the sooner she'd be able to differentiate between the two. She got dressed and focused on the day ahead. She hadn't a clue what was in store, but determination motivated her.

The influence of her enemies had to stop, and only she could stop them.

By becoming a Crystal Goddess.

Kade dressed and left his guest room in search of food. He hadn't seen Destiny since the accidental group orgasm the other night. It wasn't that he was avoiding her, but he thought she'd learn faster without the distraction of seeing him.

Not that he could get the image of the girl out of his mind. She haunted him day and night. This new, erotic version of Dr. Destiny Rue, no longer wearing that frightened expression. She'd grown in the last few days.

And he had two days left for her to heal his brother and free him.

And then?

He would present her to the Ash Demon hierarchy, who would in turn hand her over to the Grigori. He'd made a promise to Pagroe's brother.

A promise to control her, then betray her.

Bastard.

No, this was the way of Ash. His way.

He wondered how much she knew, if she'd been lucid when he'd bargained with Pagroe's brother to turn her over to the Grigori. A part of him hoped she knew what was to come, that she could prepare herself for battle.

What are you thinking, demon? She is your enemy.

Yet thinking of her that way felt wrong, especially since her physical presence eased the unrest he usually felt when inside his mortal skin.

He wandered out of the north wing, through the hallways of the manor. This time he noticed the high ceilings, the rich wood paneling trimmed in intricately carved moldings. Thick Persian carpets lined the floor, and soft lights showcased a few romantic paintings.

Romance. He'd have to romance Destiny to get what he wanted. He'd have to seduce her, gentle her with a lover's touch.

He stretched out his neck. It was going to be a long two days.

Ambling toward the library, he figured he'd distract himself by reading while she trained during the day. In the evening, he'd carry out his seductive measures, drawing her closer, developing her emotional dependence on him. He should be in full control of the Crystal Goddess in two days' time.

He still couldn't believe he'd gotten his strength back after the taxing two days on his mortal body. There was something about the manor that helped him heal. Or was it Destiny's presence? Her love?

He grew light-headed and stumbled against the wall for support. As he struggled to breathe, he felt a sudden electrical charge in the air: house demons. The creatures swirled around him like ribbons of smoke. Damn, if they sensed his true plan to control the girl, they'd expose him and he'd be crystallized for sure. His chest tightened as he sensed ethereal claws reach for him.

"Why are you here, Ash?" they howled.

"To help the Crystal Goddess."

Menacing laughter echoed off the walls. "*You* will help *her?*"

"I have protected her," he ground out against the pain. His mortal heart muscle constricted as they probed him for the truth.

Fine. He'd give them a truth to titillate and distract.

"She needs a talented Ash to do her sexual bidding. When she begs me to mate, I will surrender to her darkest desires."

"Aah. Yes…"

"I have no wish to harm her, only to pleasure her."

"Sex, sex to please the goddess." They hushed.

The claws extricated themselves from his chest and he gasped.

"Go and be her servant." The wisp of smoke drifted back up to the ceiling. "Yeeesss," they hissed. "Gooo."

It took him a second to regain his equilibrium. He'd done it. He'd convinced house demons he meant Destiny no harm, that he was here to be her sex slave.

But he would make her *his* slave. Without feeling or concern for her, he would dominate and control her gift.

He shook off the distasteful experience and started down the hallway.

"Stop! Damn it!" Destiny cried.

Once again he found himself rushing to help her. Kade stopped outside the doorway to the healer's room.

"I can't do this!" Destiny said.

"It's the first day you've tried the exercise," Edwina coached. "Give yourself time."

"I don't have time. They're still whispering inside my head."

"You are going through a great change, and that makes you vulnerable. What are they saying?"

"That they're coming for me. That they're already here, inside the castle."

"You know that's not true."

"Rationally I know it, but that doesn't seem to be helping right now."

"You need to learn to shut out the sound. Here, sit cross-legged on the cushion and hold one of these stones in each hand. There, that's right. The labradorite to absorb some of the negative energy, and the rose quartz to calm your anxiety and release the flow of love. Clear your mind, that's it."

"I can't do this," she muttered.

"You've already done it when you healed Kadenshar. Twice now."

"What do you mean?"

"On the plane—Mersey told me how you healed his wound with your rose quartz crystal. You helped me heal him that evening with the ground malachite powder. It's never worked that quickly before. You have a gift, Destiny. You must trust yourself. Can you feel the energy in your palms? How you are both protected and calmed in an energy field around you?"

"I… Yes."

"Close your eyes," Edwina instructed.

Kade couldn't help but peek into the room to watch.

"What do you see?" Edwina asked.

"Lights, like a kaleidoscope."

"Good, fine. Now open your eyes and focus on the lavender plant. Making it well, healing its disease."

"Do I need to chant?"

"Not necessarily. Focus, that's it."

Kade gripped the doorjamb. A tingling sensation filled his chest, but not a knifing pain like the assault from the house demons.

What was happening to him?

"Let the light energy fill your heart. Healing energy…that's right."

Kade took a deep breath. Then another. He didn't feel light-headed exactly. More as if his mortal body hummed with energy.

"Good, Destiny, that's it," Edwina said, circling her. "Now look at the plant."

"Oh, my God," Destiny said. "I did it. I heard the negative whispers, but I simply let them drift past. I filled my heart with healing light and I brought the plant back to life."

Edwina glanced up and spotted Kade.

"Good morning, Kadenshar," she said.

Destiny got to her feet and went to him, placing

her hand on his arm. "Hey, how are you? Feeling okay?"

He was beyond okay when she showed him such affection. When she touched him, his lungs filled with air, his heart beat a little stronger.

"I'm better, thank you."

She smiled and he glanced across the room, unable to withstand the trust in her eyes. Or was it something else? Was it the pull he felt in his chest? Were his Ash defenses so weakened that she was able to embed herself into his heart?

No, not possible.

"This is a training session, Kadenshar," Edwina said.

"Sorry to interrupt." He welcomed the excuse to leave.

"Actually, I was going to invite you to stay," Edwina offered.

"Great, so I can embarrass myself in front of an audience?" Destiny said.

Edwina picked up the potted plant. Its leaves were green and full of life. "You call this an embarrassment?"

Destiny shrugged, then looked at Kade. "You're really all right?"

"Worn out, but fine."

"Yeah, I'm tired, too. I had the weirdest dreams last night."

Kade cleared his throat and glanced at Edwina, who studied the plant in her hand.

"What?" Destiny said.

Had she read his thoughts, the desire still brewing beneath the surface?

"Continue your training," he encouraged. "We'll talk later."

She nodded and went back to sit on the purple velvet cushion.

He left the healing room and hesitated outside the door, searching the hall for more house guardians. Destiny continued with another exercise, but frustration seemed to block her. He pressed his back against the paneled wall.

"It worked before," Destiny protested. "What am I doing wrong?"

"It's a succeed-and-fail process, Destiny. Draw on your patience to get you through."

"But we have no time. Kade's brother—"

"Stop. This is not just about Kade's brother."

"I'm the only one who can save him."

"Yes. In time."

"We don't have time!"

Her words were born of frustration, as if she truly cared about Tendaeus, wanted him healthy and released. Even though he was a threat to her.

She's not thinking of herself, Kadenshar, she's thinking of you.

Fine. Perfect. Exactly as he'd planned it. At this moment he had more control over her than the Cadre did.

He pushed away from the wall and went into the library. The house demons were nowhere in sight.

Good, he must have been officially cleared of suspicion, which would make his goal a whole lot easier to attain.

The library was grand, to be sure. He must be feeling better because today he noticed things he hadn't before. One side of the room was completely covered with bookcases holding every size and style of novel. Antique vases and ceramic and glass sculptures gave the room a sophisticated feel. A leather-bound book atop the marble fireplace caught his eye. He picked it up and read the title: *The Legends and Prophecies of St. Yve Wood.*

Settling down in a wingback chair, he wondered what lies had been printed about Ash Demons. The chapter on Ash traced the existence back to the great fire of Rome, Nero's ego-driven genocide and the creatures spawned from the ashes. "Ash Demons, being created from mortal flesh and bone, would always feel at odds with their own kind and mortals," he read.

Ridiculous. He read on.

From the Ash race will come a warrior gifted with the ability to feel and embrace true compassion. He will rise above the rest and, in collaboration with the Crystal Goddess, bring balance to the dark and mortal realms.

Fairy tales. Different groups didn't connect and work together. He leaned against the wingback chair and wished for his father's presence. He could use his advice and encouragement that Kade was following the right course.

What other course could there be? Once Destiny released his brother, Kade would turn her over to his people. His loyalty was obvious and clear.

Destiny. He slowed his breathing, feeling relieved yet groundless when out of her presence. Why was that? Because he felt safe, as if he belonged beside her?

Had she inadvertently cast a spell on him? He must consider the possibility. Then he remembered the sincerity in her eyes; she was not tricking him. She truly cared.

She was falling in love with him.

All the better. He'd be able to control her if she loved him, control the witch whose mother was the cause of his father's and brother's deaths.

Yet understanding filled his heart. Her mother had run from Kade's father because she'd been trying to protect her child. She'd loved her daughter just as his father had loved Kade. Yet Ash Demons were incapable of loving.

Or so he'd been taught. To love was to be more mortal-like than demon. And Kade had a demon heart.

But even now he struggled against the compassion that opened his heart to the light-haired beauty destined to be the Crystal Goddess of legend.

He slammed the book shut and started for the

door, needing to get away, leave the manor, escape from her seductive light energy.

Edwina suddenly appeared in the doorway, blocking his path.

"Kadenshar?"

"I must leave."

"Why?"

"Are you my keeper?"

"I need to speak with you."

"And I need to leave this place." He stepped around her.

"It's about Destiny."

He hesitated. "I don't care."

"But you do. And she cares for you."

That pull, that pressure filled his chest again. He turned on Edwina. "What have you done to me, witch? You've cast some kind of love spell?"

"No. What you're feeling is the healing of—" she paused "—your soul."

"Ash Demons do not have souls and we don't feel compassion."

"Let me explain it another way. You are finding balance, becoming a higher, more evolved being."

"You mean I'm becoming mortal!"

"No, I didn't say that."

"Out of my way." He pushed past her and started for the front door.

"Destiny needs you."

He couldn't allow himself to care about the girl. Yet he couldn't bring himself to leave.

"What is this?" He turned to her. "Another spell you've cast?"

"It's not a spell. It's something I've figured out. She needs you to help develop her skills."

"Bah! Now it is you who is insane."

"Listen to me. She connects to the crystal force without effort when she's in your presence. I'm not sure if it's that the Ash leave her alone when you're around or if there's something growing between you."

"You are mistaken."

"I noticed it when we healed your knife wound and again when you stood in the doorway and she was able to heal the dying plant. For some inexplicable reason, you are her conduit to the crystal energy. She cannot learn and grow to her full potential without your help. Which means…"

"My brother is lost to me."

"No, she can heal him—but not without your help, your…" She hesitated.

"Do not say love. I will be sick."

"You needn't love her in return. But, yes, I sense that her feelings for you are empowering her. I doubt she'll need you indefinitely, but for now, for the next week, you can help her."

"We don't have a week. Ash will come for her in two days." Why in Lucifer's name did he tell her that?

Edwina nodded as if she weren't surprised that he'd so freely shared that bit of news. "I was afraid of that," she said. "I'm surprised Destiny has eluded them this long. There is something about her, her latent power perhaps, that attracts Ash Demons."

"Yes," he said. "I've noticed."

First her friend Adam, when he fought Kade for her affection, and then Pagroe when he wanted to possess her on the plane.

And, to some degree, Kade.

Every time she got close, every time she touched him, he wanted something he could not name; he burned for it.

"But you are able to resist her, aren't you?" Edwina questioned.

"I am."

"Yes, it makes sense," she whispered, then glanced up at him. "You must help her. Come." The woman turned and walked away as if confident he'd follow.

Did he have a choice? He must give of himself to help the girl reach her full potential.

But to pretend to return her feelings of love, an emotion he was incapable of feeling?

Then what is it you feel for your brother?

He caught up to the teacher. "I will help." He paused. "For my brother."

"Of course."

They turned the corner and walked into the healer's room.

"Destiny?" Edwina said.

The girl was gone.

"My god, they've got her." She grabbed Kade's arm. "Ash Demons have taken her."

Chapter 12

They wouldn't dare. He'd promised them the girl in three days. Why would they have kidnapped her?

Because they didn't believe him. Pagroe's brother must have sensed Kade's lying heart when he said he'd bring her to the Grigori.

Oh, he'd bring her back—but begrudgingly.

The teacher gripped his shirt. "Where would they have taken her? Where!"

"Dark realm. Grigori council."

Edwina raced past him down the hall.

Too late. It was too late for Destiny, too late to save his brother.

How could Ash have found the manor and then

taken her without alarm? St. Yve was invisible to all but Cadre members, and surely either the gargoyle monsters or house guardians would have stopped unwelcome Ash soldiers before they got to her. No, this was not Ash Demons' work.

"Edwina, stop!" he called. "They do not have her."

She spun around. "You're lying."

"Am I?"

She clenched her jaw.

"What was she doing when you left her to find me?" he asked.

"Practicing a medicus crystal spell."

"Which does what?"

"Allows her to heal a demon inside a crystal."

"Where are the crystals stored?"

She hesitated. It was obvious an Ash Demon roaming free in the crystal chamber was against Cadre policy.

"Either you trust me or you don't," he said. "Decide. Now."

"The dungeon. Follow me." She raced down the hall to a large steel door. With trembling fingers, she punched in an access code and the door clicked open.

What was the girl trying to do? And what if she failed? Would she unleash the demons imprisoned in the crystals, most of them deservedly imprisoned?

How could he think this of his own kind?

Down they went, deeper into the bowels of the

manor, following a long, narrow hallway. The dungeon was cool and quiet with stone walls that gave it an ancient, sinister feel.

In the distance, a body lay crumpled on the floor, but Kade felt in his heart that it was not Destiny. He sighed with relief as Edwina kneeled beside a young man.

"Squire Callahan?" she whispered.

The boy opened his eyes. "Miss Edwina? Where…?" He glanced down the hallway. "Where did she go?"

"Who?"

"The beauty with golden hair and blue eyes."

"She was here?"

"Needed to get into the crystal storage chamber. I…I didn't mean to give her the access spell, but she kissed my cheek and I couldn't help myself."

"Okay, it's okay. Stay here."

She got up and raced down the hall, Kade right beside her.

Destiny was close. Kade could tell by the tightness in his chest, the same feeling he experienced when protecting her from the Ash soldiers and when watching her practice her healing exercise.

Yet panic settled low. He instinctively knew something was wrong. Edwina chanted a quick verse, and the door to the crystal chamber swung open.

Destiny lay motionless on the floor.

"Oh, my god." Edwina kneeled beside her. "Her pulse is racing."

Kade realized he was kneeling beside her as well. Destiny's eyes were open, but she didn't speak. Her skin had paled and her lower lip trembled slightly. Kade struggled to think past the emotions jamming his thoughts.

She couldn't be dead, not that sweet girl…

…who loved him.

"Destiny—God, no, what happened to you?" Edwina asked.

"I happened to her." Pagroe stepped out of the shadows.

"Pagroe?" Kade said.

With a snap of his wrist, Pagroe tossed Kade across the room into a cabinet of crystals. The cabinet crashed to the ground, littering the stone floor with crystals of all shapes and sizes, some breaking into pieces.

"You fool! What are you doing?" Kade ground out, getting to his feet.

"Only weak demons end up in these," Pagroe said. "They are not worthy to call themselves Ash."

Where was Tendaeus? Among the shards littering the floor?

"How did you get out?" Edwina demanded.

"Your lovely girl released me."

"I don't believe you," she said.

"I don't care." Pagroe smiled.

Kade took a ready stance. His body had been weakened by what he'd endured the last few days, but he wouldn't lose to this arrogant demon.

Kade wouldn't give up on saving his brother.

Or Destiny.

"Do you want to know how I seduced her?" Pagroe said, skulking the perimeter of the room. "I impersonated your brother and tricked her into releasing me. She would do anything to earn your love, Kadenshar. She is such a pathetic, weak creature."

With a fling of his arm, Pagroe shot a bolt of black lightning at Kade. He managed to deflect it from himself and a nearby shelf of crystals. Kade apported into the hallway, hoping to draw Pagroe away from Destiny.

Pagroe started for him, then hesitated over her lifeless body.

Edwina whispered, placed a stone in Destiny's hand and closed her fingers around it.

"What do you say, witch?" Pagroe grabbed Edwina by the neck.

Kade flung himself between them and broke the hold, pinning Pagroe to the ground.

"You choose to protect a mortal witch over your own kind? They have you completely under their spell," Pagroe growled.

"She will teach the girl to heal my brother."

Pagroe flung Kade off him and howled with laughter. A maniacal, evil sound that shot chills across Kade's shoulders.

"Your brother? They told you he is still alive? And you believed them?"

Kade held his ground but didn't answer.

"You are a complete fool," Pagroe said. "They use your mortal feelings to control you and make you fight your own kind. You are but a worthless, weak Ash."

Pagroe flung Kade against another cabinet, but he managed to hold it up, saving the demons locked inside.

"I will not be fooled by their lies!" Pagroe shouted. "I will show her I am the strongest Ash, and she will beg to mate with me. I know of the prophecy—an Ash warrior will mate with a Crystal Goddess, and together they will rule!"

"They will bring balance and peace, not destroy with evil," Edwina shot back.

Kade couldn't believe it. The myth was true?

"You lie, witch!" Pagroe stepped toward her, but Kade blocked his way.

"You still protect her? They continue to lie to you, Kadenshar. And you believe them? Are you smitten with this crystal whore?"

Help me, Kadenshar. Believe in me.

It was Destiny's voice. He snapped his attention to her. She remained unconscious, yet he could feel her thoughts.

"Let me save my brother, Pagroe," Kade said. "Then you can have the girl."

I need to buy us time, my sweet, he answered her.

"She cannot save your brother. He is already dead. Tell him the truth, witch!" Pagroe grabbed Edwina by the hair.

"Let me go!" She fought against him.

"Tell him or I will kill the girl!"

"Yes, your brother is gone!"

Kade stepped back in shock. Tendaeus was dead?

He is not lost to us, Kadenshar. I can bring him back. Believe in me.

A pressure in his chest grew to a sharp pain. He clutched the material of his silk shirt. Something squeezed at his heart, forcing it to pump harder, faster.

"You believe me, brother." Pagroe let go of Edwina and she scrambled to Destiny's side.

"I do," Kade lied.

"Then you agree I am the more intelligent demon since I exposed their lies. I am king of Ash Demons!"

Pagroe sounded psychotic, irrational. Had the demon gone mad?

"King of the Ash!" He started for Destiny.

"King of Ash Demons!" Kade repeated.

With a sudden cry, Destiny sat up and pointed a crystal pyramid at Pagroe.

"You fool, you think you can hurt me with that glass?" Pagroe flung his hand, but no lightning bolt shot from his fingertips.

"Help me, Kadenshar," Destiny said. "Touch me so I can finish this."

Kade glanced at Pagroe, as helpless as a mortal, then back to Destiny, her arm trembling as she aimed the crystal point at her enemy.

Kade reached out to her.

"You would betray your own kind?" Pagroe accused. "What are you—mortal?"

"I am a brother."

"You have lost—to...them!"

Pagroe lunged.

Kade touched her shoulder and she cried, *"Te vincio!"*

Blinding golden light flashed and a high-pitched wail pierced his eardrums. He squeezed her shoulder to make sure he wouldn't break the connection.

Suddenly it was dark. A soft mist rose from the crystal in her palm.

"It's done." She glanced into his eyes. "Thank you."

He slipped his hand from her shoulder. Guilt tore at his chest for having betrayed his own kind.

"He was consumed with his own ego," she said. "He would have destroyed everything, even your brother, to feed his addiction."

"My brother is...dead, isn't he?"

Destiny held his gaze, her blue eyes round and sincere. "He's not lost to us, Kadenshar. I can bring him back. With your help."

It dawned on him how she spoke with such authority and confidence.

Don't get lured in.

"You lied to me," he said.

"No, I did not know about your brother's condition until a few minutes ago when I found his crystal.

At least I thought it was his crystal. Then Pagroe manipulated my thoughts and I touched his crystal as well. That's when he escaped."

"My brother…" He glanced at the shattered crystals on the floor.

She pulled a clear quartz pyramid from a pouch at her waist. "He's safe. With time and training, we will save him. Together."

Yet Kadenshar knew they had little time.

"How do I know I can trust you?" he said.

She pushed up on tiptoe and kissed his cheek. "You know."

Truth filled his heart. And something else.

He took a step back. "What kind of hold do you have over me, woman?"

"None. You are free to do as you please."

Strange, he didn't feel free. He felt intrinsically and desperately connected to this female.

"It would please me to free my brother and be on my way," he said.

Pain flashed in her eyes. "Then we'd better get started."

The training was more like torture.

After hours of Dee memorizing crystals and their uses, she and Kadenshar were required to meditate together. One minute his energy warmed her skin like the sun on a ninety-degree day; the next, a chill besieged her.

A shiver ran down her arms.

Focus.

"Clear your mind of all thought," Edwina coached.

Instead of floating in a bubble of light, Dee found herself lying naked at the hands of Kadenshar. She pictured him running determined masculine fingers up her stomach to her rib cage, hesitating long enough to make her arch for him.

What do you want, my sweet? he crooned. *This?*

He cupped her breasts, then rubbed his palms against her nipples, making them peak with wanting.

She snapped her eyes open. Kadenshar was smiling at her.

"Stop it," she said.

He raised a brow.

"Destiny?" Edwina questioned.

"I can't focus if he's trying to seduce me."

Edwina scowled at Kade.

"I did no such thing," he said with a hand to his chest in an innocent gesture.

"She's picking up on something floating around in your subconscious, Kadenshar," Edwina said. "Here, focus on this calcite crystal sphere. Stare at it and focus on the many bands running throughout. Our objective is to keep you from thinking about Destiny."

He focused on the crystal.

Edwina nodded for Dee to continue. She closed her eyes and inhaled the scent of sage that permeated the room. Dee hummed the *om* sound to pull her deeper into her state of psychic awareness.

"Relax your shoulders, that's right. Breathe in…and out… Now your arms, down…down, arm muscles relaxing as the light energy filters down to your fingertips."

Dee felt something cool and small placed in each palm she had rested on her knees. Crystals.

"Now I will add sound…"

Soothing flute music filled the room with a pleasing, relaxing melody that allowed her to focus on the cool stones in her hands.

Dee drifted deeper, welcoming images that floated by, not holding on to anything in particular.

Then the image of a little boy fighting against his mother's embrace drifted past.

She grabbed it. Analyzed it.

It's my fault! he shouted.

Do not say that. The mother struggled to hold him, but he fought her.

Let me go!

They died trying to save you. Make them proud that they gave their lives. Become the great leader your father always said you would be.

No! the boy cried. He wrenched away from his mother and raced into a dark black tunnel. Surrounded by black, he wasn't scared but angry and hateful. Then he came out the other side and found himself at the ledge of a great cliff overlooking miles of deep canyons.

Dee's heart raced. *Go back, go back to your mother.*

Instead the boy jumped from the cliff.

Dee threw herself after him and soared like an eagle, catching him before he hit the ground. With the boy in her arms, she landed on a mound of green grass and held him close. *To be loved is a gift.*

It is a curse! the boy sobbed.

No, feel my love.

She placed her hand over his heart.

Enough!

Jerked out of her meditation, she struggled to get her bearings.

Kadenshar towered over her. "You cannot heal me, woman. Do not try."

"I… But…" she stammered.

"I'm taking a walk." Kade stormed out of the meditation room.

Edwina settled next to Dee on the floor. "What happened?"

"A boy," she said, catching her breath. "He was devastated."

"You must have seen Kadenshar."

"I tried to comfort him. I told him to feel my love."

Edwina helped Dee to her feet. "Go find him, talk to him. You two need each other right now."

Clutching her rose quartz necklace, Destiny hurried out of the room in search of him. He wouldn't have left the manor, would he? It was too dangerous out there with Ash Demons now his enemies, along with whatever other dark forces wanted to control Dee's powers. They would all blame Kade for not destroying her.

But he needed her to save his brother's life.

No, it was more than that.

She found him in the library, staring out the tall beveled glass. With a gentle heart she came up beside him. "I didn't mean to upset you. I'm sorry."

"A week ago it all made sense," he started, not looking at her. "I was an Ash Demon warrior, destined to lure mortals into destroying themselves with their own egos. Now I find that I am the one to be destroyed."

"Why do you say that?" She touched his arm.

He glared at her fingers, but he didn't pull away.

"After you are through with me—you and your teacher—I will have no place in the dark realm. I will have betrayed my kind and will be destroyed." He sighed. "At least my brother shall live."

"It wasn't your fault," she suddenly said.

He took a step away from her to break contact. "What did you say?"

"Your father and brother—it wasn't your fault."

"You know nothing of it." He started for the door.

"They loved you. Just as my mother loved me."

He spun on her and closed the distance between them. Gripping her arms, his green eyes flared. "Ash do not feel love."

"I've read about Ash Demons. They are more like mortals than any other creature. Your father loved you. That is why he sought help. You love your brother—"

"No, I am responsible for him."

"You love him. And we will save him, together, if you stop wasting time with all this guilt you carry."

"You know nothing of it."

"No? My mother spent her life in a mental hospital with crazy people in order to protect me. They drugged her and strapped her down when she feigned insanity. I know guilt, Kadenshar. Don't add to yours by losing your brother, too. Come on, we have to get back to work."

When she took his hand, she thought he might pull away. Instead his grip tightened as if he needed the connection, craved it. She started walking, and to her surprise, he walked alongside her, quiet and pensive. Neither spoke for the rest of the afternoon's session.

That night she lay in bed, restless, wondering where he slept.

Wishing he'd come to her.

It wasn't a mere wish.

More like an ache that started low in her belly and worked its way through her body, filling her blood with lust.

Had a lust demon sneaked its way into the manor? No, the guardians were incredibly efficient creatures. This ache originated from within. Could it be she was falling in love with Kadenshar?

More like she intuitively knew she needed him to complete her training.

And then?

She'd heal his brother, release him, and Kade would be out of her life.

Lust dissolved into emptiness. Alone her entire life, these few days were the first she could remember feeling tied to someone. Feeling connected.

Feeling a comfortable companionship.

She should enjoy the feeling while it lasted.

Someone knocked softly on her door and she ignored it. She didn't want to talk to anyone or have to force a smile.

Her visitor knocked again. Maybe it was Mersey coming to check on her.

Dee got out of bed and unlocked her door, cracking it open. Her breath caught at the sight of Kadenshar, wearing a white cotton shirt open in front and trim slacks. He held an oil lantern.

"Uh-oh, you heard me?" she said.

"Heard you? No, I thought I heard Lady Aurora's voice. I can't risk her finding me. Your teacher went to the city to find her and explain the situation. They must have crossed paths."

"Come in." She pulled him across the threshold.

"I'm sorry if I awakened you."

"You didn't."

"Sleep eludes you?"

"Yes. You?"

"I don't sleep, not much."

She shifted on the edge of the bed as he sat in the chair by the window. He was keeping his distance. Why?

"Is that a demon thing, not sleeping?" she asked.

"I don't think so."

She fiddled with the eyelet lace bedcover. "Do you want to sleep?" She glanced up at him.

He looked delicious with his hair hanging loose across his shoulders and his shirtsleeves rolled up.

"Sleep is overrated, I'm sure," he said.

"Maybe, but not what comes before it."

Their eyes locked.

God, I wish this man would make love to me.

"Tell me you didn't hear that," she said.

He smiled.

She flopped back against the bed. "I'm so embarrassed." She shoved a pillow over her reddened face.

The bed shifted and he slipped the pillow off her face.

"I will sleep," he said. "But we shouldn't—"

She pulled him down to kiss her, wrapping her arms around his neck, wanting more, wanting all of him. When she touched his naked chest he moaned with need. Wetness pooled between her legs as she arched against his hard, warm body. She couldn't stand much more. She needed him inside her.

He broke the connection. "I can't." He breathed heavily against her.

"Why not?"

"If we mate before your thirtieth birthday, it could affect your powers. I will not do that to you."

"Because you need me to save your brother—I get it."

He stared into her eyes. "No, because you could be vulnerable to those who fear you. I will not do that to you."

"Why not?"

He broke eye contact and glanced toward the window. With her fingers to his cheek, she guided his attention back to her. "Because you care about me?" she whispered.

He clenched his jaw.

"Kadenshar?"

"I care. I shouldn't."

She'd read of demon possession, how they could leave their essence in a mortal's body to influence their thoughts and actions.

Kadenshar could control her, but he chose not to. Because he cared about her.

And she loved him. She closed her eyes. This couldn't be a good thing.

He pulled away. "You are upset with me. I will leave."

She touched his arm. "No, don't. Lie here with me. Sleep with me."

He glanced at the door.

"Please?" she said. "I've been alone for so long."

And she sensed that time was running out. By tomorrow evening she would be ready to attempt healing and releasing his brother.

She ached to sleep one night in Kade's arms.

Pulling back the covers, she patted the bed beside her. "Take your shirt off and lie on your stomach."

He eyed her speculatively and then did as ordered. She suspected this was a first for him—lying beside a woman but not having sex with her.

As he stretched out beneath the covers, she reached for her amethyst wand on the nightstand and placed the rounded end to his spine. The other end, the crystal point, would draw imbalance away from his body, helping him sleep. She rubbed gently, back and forth, humming softly, she wasn't sure why.

"That feels…good," he said.

She continued her healing treatment, hoping to ease the guilt that tortured his conscience. Yet how would she be able to keep her hands off his hard, solid muscles, and her lips away from his warm, inviting ones?

A snoring sound vibrated from the bed.

"You've fallen asleep on me," she whispered with a smile.

He felt comfortable and safe enough to fall asleep beside her. Her heart warmed. She placed the wand back on the nightstand and turned down the oil lamp.

She slipped beneath the covers and edged her body beside his, placing his arm protectively across her.

She loved him. God help her. She'd fallen in love with a demon. What on earth was to become of her?

Chapter 13

Destiny awakened and went in search of the perfect spot in the woods to start her work. Something had driven her out here to a healing pond near a powerful ley line: the pond she'd seen in her visions.

As she ambled down a pebbled trail, she sensed the otherworldly creatures of the enchanted forest were fascinated by her but not frightened. Ash Demon voices were becoming a thing of the past since her growing protective energy repelled their destructive whispers.

Something had happened during the night, a transformation that she couldn't explain. When she'd glanced into the mirror this morning she'd hardly recognized herself. She looked wiser, more confident and at peace. Her blond hair shimmered as it hung wildly about her shoulders. Her lips glowed a natural pink-rose.

She'd awakened a healer, thanks to Kade's love. They'd held each other through the night but did not need to have sex to feel the strength of the light energy flowing between them.

Their love fed the power within her. And she knew what she had to do.

With Tendaeus's crystal tucked safely in her pouch at her waist, she followed the path deeper into the woods, using instinct to guide her. About ten minutes later she happened upon the healing pond. She disrobed and, clutching the crystal in her left hand, immersed herself in the welcoming waters.

She meditated, humming a soft chant to balance her energies. The rose quartz around her neck warmed her skin as she focused on slowing her breath, riding the wave of light energy that filled her heart.

She sensed the creatures of the enchanted forest watching her, intrigued by the spiritual aura of a crystal healer. It was as if they had been expecting her for many years.

Tendaeus's crystal burned her palm as she dipped it into the water, but she clung tight. This was Kade's brother; she loved Kade and would do anything for him.

"Crystal glow…ease the strain…heal his wounds…release his pain."

She repeated the words until she felt the energy shift. He was no longer dead, but he was not healed either. Pain radiated from the crystal into her hand and up her arm. She struggled to hold on to it, calming her breath, shutting out the burn in her palm. She grew light-headed and decided to place it back into her pouch.

Kadenshar's brother might be healed physically, but mentally he was broken and sick. If she released him now, she feared the carnage he'd inflict on the peaceful paras of the woods and the people living at the manor.

She wanted to help him, heal him.

You can't heal those who choose to suffer.

Closing her eyes, she realized it was her own intuition that spoke to her.

She skimmed the surface of the healing pond with her fingertips. Warmth drifted up her arms to her shoulders, relaxing the muscles there. The stress of the past few days had settled heavily against her neck and shoulders. The healing pond eased her burden and lightened her heart.

All she ever wanted was to help others and be loved.

You are a healer and you are loved.

She wouldn't be loved by the one who counted most if she couldn't heal his brother.

True love is unconditional. True love is eternal.

"Right," she muttered. A sudden chill made her open her eyes.

There, blocking the sunlight, stood Kadenshar, dressed in all black, a slight curve to his lips as he eyed her naked body.

"I awakened to an empty bed," he said. "I was worried."

"How did you find me?"

"I don't know."

But she did. They were connected in a way that defied rational explanation.

"I'm sorry about leaving you this morning." She stepped out of the pond. He took her hand and pulled her up against him, but her desire was tempered with concern. She wanted him. Forever. But he would be gone soon enough, once his brother was free.

She pulled her hand from his and dried off with a towel, then slipped into her loose-fitting tunic and pants. "I wanted to get started early on your brother's healing."

"How is he?"

"He's alive. The healing waters brought him back."

"No, you brought him back." With a forefinger and thumb, he tipped her face to look into his eyes.

She wanted to cry.

"What is it?" he said.

"You know me so well."

"I'd like to know you better." He smiled.

"Yes, well, in good time." She interlaced her hand in his and they took the path back to the manor. She'd enjoy their few moments of tenderness while she could.

"You didn't answer me," he said.

"What was the question?" She couldn't look at him.

"What is bothering you?"

"A lot's happened to me in the last week." She sighed. "I went from a rational scientist to an insane victim of mental torture to a powerful crystal healer. I'm still trying to get my bearings."

He cupped her shoulders. "Are you…do you mean you've made the transition to Crystal Goddess?"

The hope in his eyes broke her heart. His only interest was that, as a Crystal Goddess, she could save his brother.

Actually, she couldn't. No one could save a determined mind, and she was getting the impression his brother's mind was hardened with resentment and hatred.

"I'm not a goddess yet—but soon," she lied, motioning for him to walk beside her. No reason to tell him what she'd learned; maybe she could still heal Tendaeus's black heart.

Doubtful. In her heart she feared she lied to Kadenshar so she could enjoy his company a little longer.

As they ambled out of the forest, she enjoyed the sounds of nature and the peace it brought her. Once they went inside the manor he would press her for answers about his brother.

She wasn't ready for that.

Would he even believe her?

Edwina waited at the front door. "Where have you been?"

"I found a healing pond in the woods."

"It's dangerous for you out there."

"Not anymore."

Edwina eyed her.

"I'm fine," Destiny assured. "But hungry."

They went to the kitchen, where a cake with brightly lit candles filled the table.

"What's this?" Destiny asked.

"It's your birthday."

"No, it's not for another month."

"Actually, today, April twenty-first, is your birthday. The May birthday was created to confuse your enemies."

Destiny was stunned. "So I'm thirty today?"

"Yes, and you can't lose your powers, no matter what happens." Edwina glanced at Kadenshar and then at the floor in embarrassment.

Aunt Edwina must have sensed the desire arcing between them. Her birthday. She was now thirty. She could have sex with anyone and not be harmed.

But she didn't want to have sex with anyone.

She wanted Kade to make love to her. Love, not sex.

"Will you continue to work on my brother?" he asked.

Whereas her mind had drifted to them making love, Kade's had been focused on his brother. Sure, right. She had to accept the fact he didn't love her.

"I will continue working on him," she said. "After cake."

"Very well." He turned to leave.

"You're not staying?" Dee asked.

"I have some business to attend to. I'll meet you in the healing room…when?"

She glanced at the wall clock. It read one in the afternoon. She had no idea she'd been in the healing pool all morning.

"Three o'clock is fine," she said.

"Until then." With a nod he disappeared.

"I'll cut you a piece," Edwina offered.

"I'm not hungry."

"But you said…"

"Okay, maybe I am hungry."

"Stop. Focus. What is going on in that pretty head of yours?" Her aunt searched her eyes.

"I'm there, Edwina. I've reached my full potential. Because of him." She motioned over her shoulder toward the door.

"What…? I don't understand."

"I love him. And it's not a spell, not his demon influence. It's love."

"My God," she whispered. "So the prophecy is true."

"What prophecy?"

"The one about a Crystal Goddess and an Ash Demon joining forces to bring peace and balance to the universe."

"Not this demon. He doesn't love me, can't love me."

Especially since I won't give him what he wants most: his brother's freedom.

"I disagree. I've seen the way he looks at you."

"Longingly?" Destiny stood and paced to the window. "Sure, it's longing for what I can do for him—free his brother."

"It's more than that." She came up behind her and rubbed Destiny's shoulder in a loving gesture. But the only love Destiny wanted to feel was love from Kadenshar.

"I'm going to rest," Destiny said. "I'll need it if I'm to work on his brother again."

Four hours into their afternoon session, Dee wanted to cry. Nothing she did could heal his brother's black soul. Nothing could dissolve his anger and resentment. It was almost as if he'd been infected with a black virus of hatred.

"How is it going?" Kade asked.

Now that she'd reached Goddess status she could easily keep him out of her thoughts, so he couldn't read her concern. She no longer needed Kade as her conduit to the energy, but she didn't tell him that. She'd enjoy his company as long as she could.

Until she told him the truth: that she could not, in good conscience, release his brother.

"It's slow," she said, standing.

"But he's better?"

"Yes."

And bitter, angry and violent.

"What aren't you telling me?"

Ah, he still was able to read her.

"He's not ready to be released," she said.

"Why?"

Because he's volatile, angry and dangerous.

"I'd like him to heal fully before releasing him. I've been told that the transformation from crystal to the mortal realm can be devastating to the system. We want him to be strong."

"Yes," he agreed.

"Then trust me." Her words rang hollow, even to herself.

She wrapped his brother's crystal in a soft oil-cloth and handed it to him. "You should hold on to this. He will feel your light energy, your—" She hesitated, not wanting to upset him by using the L word. "He'll sense your presence."

He took it from her. "You've given up?"

"No, I'm wiped out. I can't do anything for him tonight."

"You're keeping something from me. What?"

You mean that I've fallen in love with you or that your brother is a killer?

"I need to rest, Kadenshar," she said.

"Why do you betray me?"

She stared him down. "Says the man who promised me to the Ash Demon as bounty? You, the demon that blames my mother for his father's and brother's deaths?"

He jerked back as if slapped.

"I've seen into your heart. I know all about it. How they went to her for help, frightened her into running straight into the path of an oncoming car. If I were betraying you, I'd be well within my rights."

She took a deep breath and calmed herself.

"But healers don't work that way," she said. "I could never betray the man I love."

He didn't blink, didn't act affected in the least by her admission.

"So you've cast a spell on me, Kadenshar, a spell of eternal love. Therefore I will do everything in my power to release your brother—when he is ready."

She rushed out of the room, ignoring Mersey Bane's greeting and her aunt's announcement that dinner was ready.

Dinner? Who could eat with this frenetic energy flying about?

Love energy. Hate energy. Resentment energy.

Ah, she had to dissolve that. She shouldn't resent him for not returning her feelings.

But she did resent him. She resented the fact that he couldn't love her enough to see past his own needs and realize she ached to give him what he wanted most—his brother's freedom—but couldn't.

She marched to her room and locked the door. Why couldn't she heal Tendaeus so she could release him and send Kade on his way? She couldn't stand to be in the same room with him anymore, feeling his energy burn her skin and ignite the desire in her heart.

Desire for a man who did not love her.

Chapter 14

She loved him. Kade shifted in the leather wing-back chair and sipped his whiskey. He'd poured himself a drink right after she'd dropped that bomb and run off. But he wouldn't drink too much. He needed to be sharp to finish this.

She loved him.

Yet showed her love by betraying him? Keeping that which he wanted most away from him, like dangling a virgin in front of a lust demon?

He sensed she could release his brother but wouldn't. Why? She was keeping something from him. Or did she not want to release Tendaeus because then Kadenshar would have no reason to stay?

Not true. He had every reason to stay. He had fallen in love with the Crystal Goddess.

He'd realized as much last night, after manipulating his way into her bedroom with the lie that Lady Aurora was back. After hours of lying in each other's arms and warming each other's hearts, Kade could no longer deny the truth. And when he'd awakened to an empty pillow beside him, the ache in his chest had been overwhelming. He needed her like no other.

And he resented his dependence, his weakness.

Pouring his second shot of whiskey, he let his gaze wander to his bedroom fireplace. The embers needed to be stoked and prodded to life.

Savage saints, he loved her. He loved a creature that lied to him and betrayed him. Mortals. They were selfish, arrogant thieves, for she'd stolen his heart, to be sure.

But she would not keep his brother from him. She would not steal Kade's last chance to regain his honor.

He tossed back the shot of whiskey and stood. She needed him to develop her powers and she loved Kadenshar, which meant…

If he made love to her, he might be able to absorb her powers long enough to release his brother himself. Surely he had to try. But he'd have to seduce her first.

The thought should sicken him.

It didn't.

He cleaned up, released his hair of its bindings and changed into an outfit the house brownies had pressed for him: expensive slacks, tailored shirt and jacket. Had the small, industrious creatures that acted as servants sensed the hum of desire surrounding the couple? Anticipated this night?

With a purposeful stride, he headed for her room.

"Never go empty-handed," a voice said.

"Never empty-handed," another whispered.

And there, outside her door, sat a bottle of faerie wine. Bless those house brownies. He'd have to leave them something special tonight—a book on demon lore, perhaps? The wine was perfect. The effects of the magical brew would prevent her from reading his thoughts, his true intentions.

As he reached for the bottle, he was slammed back to the opposite wall. The house guardians were back.

"Ash Demon, what is your purpose?"

"I am at the will of the Crystal Goddess," he said with sincerity. "She calls to me. She needs my demon skill to fulfill her destiny. Sex, all night, at her bidding."

A minute passed and Kadenshar held his breath. What if they didn't believe him? Would they lock him up until Lady Aurora returned to exact her final revenge?

Focus on getting past the guardians and into her room. He calmed his breathing and cleared his thoughts…

…and imagined her sparkling blue eyes and tentative smile.

"He loves her," a voice whispered.

"Yes," the other confirmed.

They released him. He straightened the lapels of his jacket, picked up the wine and knocked on her door.

His heart raced like thundering hooves. Was he nervous? No, anxious to be done with this chore. He'd fooled the house guardians, but would he be able to fool Destiny?

He loves the healer.

Loves her.

Yes, against his own will, Kade loved her. Damn the woman.

He knocked again. Had she fallen asleep? He doubted it. Her need pulsated through the manor walls, calling to him, stirring something primal, and not just beneath his waist.

The door cracked open and he tightened his grip on the bottle at the sight of her. She'd pinned some of her hair back, but wisps of silken gold touched her bare shoulders. She wore a low-cut pale pink negligee, loose-fitting straps holding it in place. The rose quartz charm glowed at the base of her neck.

The love stone.

"You came," she said.

"You expected me?"

"I'd hoped." She pushed the door wide and

stepped back into the darkened room, as if afraid of him.

"I brought wine," he said.

"Thank you." She shot him a tentative smile and went to gaze out the window.

He stepped inside her room and shut the door, locking it. They could not be disturbed tonight.

As she stood by the window, he could see the silhouette of her naked body through her nightdress. He opened the wine, found a glass on her nightstand and poured the magical brew.

"Here, my sweet," he said, handing her the glass.

"What about you?"

"We will share," he said.

Two hearts. One love.

No! He fought against the truth.

She took the glass but did not look into his eyes. Feeling guilty, perhaps?

You're the one who should feel guilty, bastard.

"It's beautiful outside," she said.

He followed her gaze. In the distance he could see the twinkle of a faerie reel in the woods.

"Not as beautiful as you," he whispered against her long, delicious neck. He kissed her there and she tipped her head to give him better access.

This would be so easy.

"Kadenshar," she whispered.

"What, my sweet? What do you need from me?"

"To talk."

"Talk?"

Kiss.

"No talking." He put down the faerie wine bottle. He trailed his fingers beneath the meager straps and slid them off her shoulders. Her nightgown pooled at her feet.

"I need to tell you about…about your brother," she started.

He silenced her with his fingertips to her lips. "Shh. You've done so much for me, Destiny. It's my turn now. I'm going to fulfill your desire and make passionate love to you."

"But…I…"

He ran his hands down the outside of her arms, and interlacing his fingers in hers, he brought her hands up, around the back of his neck. He trailed his fingers down her sides, slowly, barely touching her skin. Down, down and around to her hip bones.

"Kade," she breathed.

"I'm here, my love."

She leaned into him, pressing her cheek against his shoulder. As he slipped his hands lower, grazing the soft curls between her legs, she arched against him.

"Open for me, my love," he said. "Give yourself to me."

Give all of yourself: your love, your honor, your magic.

She spread her legs and he stroked her ever so gently.

"My God," she whispered.

Hardly.

His cock filled with need for her, and he struggled to control his urge. He must be tender and gentle to make her willingly surrender.

He trailed his hand up past her belly button, her stomach, to cup her breasts. As he massaged and stroked, she started to slip from his grasp. She was losing her ability to stand.

With a smooth lift, he carried her to the bed and laid her on top of the covers, eyeing her beautiful naked body. He wanted to drive himself into her over and over, possessing every inch of her. He took off his jacket and tossed it to a nearby chair.

"No," she said.

"What?" Had he been caught?

"I want to undress you."

Sitting on the edge of the bed, she spread her legs to bring him close. She started with his belt buckle. Evil wench. She didn't waste time getting to the heart of things. His trousers fell to the floor. She ran her hands beneath his shirt and stood as she pulled it up, over his head and off. Running her hands across his chest, her eyes grew wide with appreciation, with wanting.

Her innocent yet ravenous gaze turned him on.

The only thing left were his silk boxers.

She slipped her fingers beneath the elastic waistband and edged them down, off his hips. When he felt her hands on him, he thought he'd go mad, lose his mind, his will to dominate her.

No, this is not one of your casual dalliances. This is the creature whose power you need.

She kissed his cock with warm, wet lips and he fought his surrender. He couldn't lose control, couldn't lose this battle.

With a groan, he took charge and pushed her back against the sheets, mounting her. Her startled expression dissolved into need, and his own need threatened to drive all thought and control from his mind. He would have this woman in time. But he needed to do it right, needed to gentle her, earn her trust so she would willingly give herself to him—her heart, her soul, her power.

He released the clip from her hair and ran his hands through the soft golden waves. She looked less innocent this way, less vulnerable.

She seemed wild, like a woman able to match his sexual prowess. And he wanted to think of her that way: as a predator he needed to tame.

Her eyes were half-closed, and the tip of her tongue darted out to moisten her lips. Was she remembering the taste of him?

Control. I must control this.

With restrained passion, he layered gentle kisses to her forehead and down, to her cheek and neck. Her fingers dug into his shoulders as if this tender act was driving her to the edge of orgasm.

I want it all, my sweet.

"Kadenshar," she breathed.

He kissed her then, tempted her with his tongue,

and her lips parted for him. Ash didn't have the usual forked tongue of other Daemon Sapiens, but they had their own magic: heat.

The kiss grew deeper as she pulled him close. But he broke the kiss, needing to tease her more. He placed her hands to the headboard and she gripped the iron bars, holding on, trying to stay grounded.

She would lose that fight.

His kisses trailed lower, between her breasts, then he laved at her nipple. The pebbled nub tasted like an exotic fruit, and as he took it between his teeth, she moaned and arched beneath him.

"What are you doing to me?" she moaned.

"Whatever you want me to do."

He circled the other breast, nipping and suckling until she cried out. "Please, Kadenshar!"

With a conquering smile, he continued kissing her, lower, past her belly button, while treasuring her breasts with his hands, rubbing and stroking the pebbled points until she cried deep in her throat.

He eased her legs apart and hesitated before tasting her. This was it; she would lose herself to him completely once his demon tongue caressed her femininity.

"Relax, my sweet," he whispered, then kissed her, the hypnotic taste of mortal mixed with crystal healer making him grow even harder with need. She tasted different than any female he'd experienced.

Different—and his.

He laved at the dewy elixir that pooled there,

wanting her to remember this night, remember his mouth on her. He would possess her, always.

"Kadenshar!" she cried out.

With a stroke of his tongue he brought her to climax. She writhed beneath him, arched and fell still. He felt her power drain from her body.

In this weakened state she would be unable to protect herself from what was to happen next. For every time he filled her with his seed, he'd take something in return—he'd steal a bit of her power.

Her breathing slowed as her body lay limp beneath him. It was his job to bring it back to life, to bring her to climax again and again.

But this time with him inside of her. He kissed his way back up her torso and straddled her, waiting.

She opened her eyes. "That was amazing."

"That was only the beginning."

Her eyes widened.

"Touch me," he commanded.

She sheathed his cock with her fingers, squeezing, stroking.

Yes, this is it. Let her feel your power, make her want it inside of her.

He licked her breast, then blew warm demon breath on the wanting peak. He grew harder, larger, and her grip grew tighter, more determined.

Want me. Crave me.

She released him and gripped his arms, digging her fingers into his mortal flesh. "Inside me," she demanded. "Now."

"As you wish, master."

The tip of his cock teased her opening, taunting her to open even wider. She wrapped her legs around his waist, giving him full access.

"Do you want me?" he asked.

"Yes."

"How much do you want me?"

"With all my heart."

"Then surrender yourself."

"Yes," she said in a hush. "Yes."

He thrust inside her and she cried out his name. But he would not give in so easily. He pulled out and with all the self-control he could muster he teased her opening again with the tip of his need.

"Please, Kadenshar!"

"Are you begging me?"

"Yes, take me."

She surrendered, she begged. And she would do it again, at least four times before sunrise. He would make sure she'd be sated and spent.

That she would be his. Completely.

He thrust and she dug her nails into his shoulders.

"Kadenshar!"

Again.

"You're mine." Satan's tears, he ached to lose himself in this woman.

"Mine."

Thrust.

I love you.

Had she thought the words or had he?

He thrust again, and light flashed behind his eyelids as his mortal senses exploded into pieces. The orgasm of a lifetime, that's what it was. His body strained with satisfaction as his mind struggled to make sense of it.

He lay next to her in bed and pulled her against his chest. Warmth flooded to every nerve ending in his body. Warmth and something else.

Her power. He could feel it seep into his soul.

But not enough. Not yet.

"Did you like that, my sweet?" he said.

"Mmm."

"Good, because I'm not finished."

They'd mated three more times during the night, each time more intense than the last. And each time he felt her light energy drain from her body—and he couldn't help but wonder if she would ever get it back.

He shouldn't care.

But he did.

He cared for this sorceress in a way he'd never cared for another creature. An odd, thrilling sensation swirled in his belly as he stroked her naked back. He'd claimed her as his own this night.

A part of him wished it was for all eternity.

But it was not to be. He had his brother to think about, the brother she refused to release from the crystal prison.

Slipping quietly out of bed, he dressed and went

to his room. Shoving aside his conscience, he locked the door and placed his brother's crystal on the windowsill. Kadenshar took a deep breath. He could feel Destiny's power surge through his body. She'd given herself freely, allowed him to take all that he'd wanted without resistance.

Guilt weighed heavily against his chest.

He must do this quickly. Remembering the release spell he'd heard Edwina teach Destiny, he began his chant. Light energy surged through him. The Cadre adepts used their own kind of power, but Destiny's was unique and intense. Could an Ash Demon survive manipulating it for his own purpose?

"Expedio!" he called out. A flash of red burst across the room; streams of bright stars exploded against the ceiling.

And there before him stood his brother.

"Tendaeus," Kade said.

His brother crossed the room and hugged Kade. "You have saved me, brother. I knew you would."

The embrace drained Kadenshar even further. His legs gave way and he collapsed on the floor. Tendaeus helped him sit up against the wall.

"You rest, brother," Tendaeus said. "I will take care of our enemies."

Kade struggled to stand, but his limbs had no strength.

"Tendaeus, we must talk. Things have changed."

He'd discovered compassion and love.

He'd fallen in love with the healer.

"There's no time for talk, brother," Tendaeus said, a twinkle in his eye. "There are many enemies to destroy. You'll join me when you regain your strength."

"Vengeance is not the way. Our father fought because he loved."

"Love? There is no such thing."

"Why do you think I released you?"

"Duty. Not love." Tendaeus knelt beside Kadenshar, his face mere inches way. "For I do not love you, Kadenshar."

His eyes were black, empty.

This was not his brother. Something inside the crystal had changed him. He'd never been cruel.

"Now, if you don't mind, I'm off to destroy this museum from the inside out. Starting with that crystal bitch."

"Listen to yourself, Tendaeus. She saved your life. And you will kill her?"

"It's a trick. All mortals are tricksters. She is but mortal with para blood running through her. An anomaly, our enemy."

"No, she is of goodness and light."

"And we are of darkness, brother. That can never change."

"This place, these people, saved you from being blasted by P-Cell. They kept you safe so that you could heal."

"They imprisoned me in a crystal. Do you have any idea what that is like? The torture I endured?"

Kade remembered Aurora's determination to inflict as much pain as possible to get what she needed out of him. But they weren't all like her.

There was Edwina and Mersey Bane.

And sweet, gentle Destiny.

"I agree, they are not all good, any more than we are all evil," Kade said, trying to get through to him. "It's about balance, Tendaeus. Our kind is more mortal than most. You must embrace your mortal side as well as the demon in you."

"No!" he howled, throwing an antique chair across the room with a mere wave of his hand. "I am a demon, an agent of darkness."

"What's happened to you?"

"I grew strong in my prison."

Kade did not recognize this creature as his brother. He sounded…psychotic.

"And now I will finish what you are too weak to do."

Kade struggled to stand, but his limbs were weak, useless. "You can't do this."

"Can't destroy the healer?" Tendaeus shot him a maniacal smile. "Have you lost your heart to her? She must be a powerful sorceress. Do not worry, brother. I will destroy her and break the bond between you. I will start by mating with her until she forgets your existence. Then I will destroy this vile place."

Tendaeus strode to the door.

"No." Kade reached for his ankle and Tendaeus kicked him in the stomach.

"She has twisted your mind, brother. But not to worry. You will be normal again soon."

He sauntered out the door, humming.

Great devil, Kade had released a monster inside Cadre walls. A monster that was going to kill Destiny.

The love of Kade's life, his reason for his existence in any realm.

With his last bit of strength, he sat up and pumped his fists. More, he needed to revive the circulation in his body, in his legs, so that they would carry him to her room. He hoped the house guardians were on alert.

He shut out the panic surging throughout his mortal veins and thought of Destiny, how she'd looked last night when he'd gone to her room.

Expectant.

In love.

Hear me, my sweet. I've made a grave mistake and danger is on its way. Wake up. Arm yourself.

He pushed up on weakened legs, adrenaline rushing through his blood, giving him strength to stand. With long, deep breaths, he focused, as he had in exercises with Destiny, and stumbled to the door. As he made his way down the hall, he spotted Tendaeus entering her room. Good, the house guardians must have detained him.

Kade reached her room and the door slammed in his face. Locked out. Unable to save her.

"Open!" he commanded, mortal adrenaline igniting his demon skill.

The door flung wide and Kade spotted Destiny sitting in the bed, hugging her knees to her chest, trembling.

"She is a beauty, Kadenshar." Tendaeus stroked her hair, mussed from their lovemaking. "I can see why you wouldn't want me to damage this temptress. You plan to keep her as a plaything?"

"Don't touch her."

"Oh, my, she has cast a powerful spell on you." Tendaeus ambled to the window. "But I will release you."

Kade started toward her and stumbled against his own weakness. Kneeling beside the bed, he said, "I made a mistake in releasing him. Please forgive me."

"A mistake?" Tendaeus cried, turning to them. "Freeing your own brother was a mistake?"

"You are sick, Tendaeus. You need help. You weren't ready to be released. I see that now."

"You see nothing!" With a jerk of his fist, he flung Kade into wooden bookshelves and he fell to the floor. "You've been bewitched by this creature's seductive magic."

Kade gasped for air. Had to save her, protect her.

I love you, he thought, in the hopes she would hear him.

But she did not take her eyes off his brother.

"You must die!" Tendaeus said, taking a step toward her.

Kade apported between them, but his brother's strength was formidable. He tossed Kadenshar aside and continued toward the bed. Kade pushed to his feet, leaning against the wall.

"I will show you what true possession is." Tendaeus was too close, only a few feet away.

"Leave her alone!" Kade called. Helpless to move, he'd do anything, even give his life for hers.

"Let's start with a kiss."

The glint of a crystal caught his eye. Destiny had heard Kade's earlier warning and had armed herself.

"Do you think that frightens me, you pathetic witch?" Tendaeus said.

She aimed and chanted, but Kade feared she didn't have the strength to crystallize him. Of course not. Kade had stripped it from her, left her defenseless.

Kade apported to her side and touched her arm. "Do it now!"

"Te vincio!"

"No!" his brother cried.

With a flash, she and Kadenshar were rocked back against the iron headboard. Struggling to breathe, he rolled off the bed and went to where his brother had stood.

"Heathen's curse!" he cried, guilt tearing him apart inside.

"What's going on?" Mersey Bane said, racing into the room and aiming a crystal at him.

"Do it!" he demanded, wanting to be put out of his misery.

He'd betrayed both his brother and the woman he loved. He deserved to be destroyed.

"Now!" he ordered.

Mersey looked to Destiny for direction.

Destiny's blue eyes misted with tears as they locked with Kade's.

"I'm sorry," she whispered and nodded to Mersey.

A flash blinded him, then nothing.

Chapter 15

Destiny had no choice. She felt Kadenshar's shame for crystallizing his brother.

She sensed his agony.

"Destiny?" Mersey said, holding the crystal in her hand.

"It was the right thing to do."

"But I thought…"

"That he cares about me?"

"Loves you."

"He does. And loving me, choosing me over his brother, would destroy him. Locking him in the crystal will keep him safe…even from himself."

"You've heard stories about what it's like to exist

in here." Mersey went to the bed and handed Dee the smoky quartz crystal.

"I will keep him close." Dee took the crystal and placed it against her heart. "He will feel my love and be safe."

"Forever?"

"No, just until I figure out how to ensure his safety."

"Well, he can't stay here for long. Lady Aurora will destroy him."

"Not if she knows that together he and I bring balance to the mortal and dark realms. It's the Grigori that concerns me. Kade gave them his word to deliver me. If he breaks it they will come for him and destroy him."

They sat in contemplative silence.

"There's only one way to solve this," Destiny said. "He must bring me to them."

"Have you gone completely round the bend? Those black lords will kill you."

"Not if destroying me will destroy their world as well. If I die at the hands of a dark realm agent, all portals to the mortal realm will disappear. Remember the prophecy about the great Crystal Goddess who will destroy the Ash Demon race? I'll prove that creatures of the dark realm are in danger of being cut off from their mortal lives if they mess with me. If I die, if I'm tortured, they will be locked in their world indefinitely—imprisoned, if you will."

"Do you think it will work?"

"It has to. I must convince them that they need me to maintain balance in both the dark and mortal realms. My healing powers will sweeten the deal."

"They don't care about healing."

"They will if it affects them." Dee stood and grabbed her robe from the armoire. It amazed her how she embraced her nakedness, not feeling self-conscious or embarrassed.

"The insanity that afflicted Tendaeus and Pagroe was an adult strain of Ash disease. Ash are the most evolved type of demon, the most humanlike and the most powerful. This disease could wipe out the entire Ash race. The Grigori would suffer from that loss."

"Can you heal them?"

"Yes. Another bargaining chip." She put Kaden-shar's crystal in a soft leather pouch and hung it around her neck. "I'm going to shower and get dressed. I need to be off before sunrise."

"We should tell Edwina."

"No, don't tell anyone." She went to Mersey and touched her shoulder, realizing how young the girl suddenly seemed.

And how old Destiny felt. Not old—wise.

"The Cadre will try to stop me, yet they are all in danger from the Grigori if I don't do this," Destiny said.

"Then I'll come with you."

Destiny smiled. "I appreciate your friendship, but I must do this alone."

But not really alone. Kade would be with her, his presence giving her power and strength.

They were the couple of the prophecy: a Crystal Goddess and a demon warrior. Together they would work to maintain balance among the mortal and dark realms. Yet she couldn't ask him to give up his identity as an Ash Demon warrior. And in her eyes he would always see his betrayal of his beloved brother.

Love. Kadenshar felt it. She'd heard him say the words in his mind after he'd made love to her.

It was love for his brother that had driven him to release Tendaeus. She wished he would have trusted his love for Destiny, believed in her enough to know she had a reason not to release his brother. But then, she was partly at fault. She hadn't confided in him about Tendaeus's condition because she hadn't wanted to break Kade's heart.

She gave Mersey a hug and sent her on her way. Destiny readied herself for her confrontation with the Grigori. She should fear them, but what she feared most was the thought of Kadenshar being hunted and tortured by his own kind.

Because of her.

Once his safety was ensured, she would leave him in the dark realm and continue her work as a healer. Sure, her heart would never be whole without Kadenshar, but she couldn't be distracted by a broken heart. There was much work to be done, mortals and paras to heal.

Now, if she could only survive her next move.

* * *

The last thing Kade remembered was crystallizing his brother.

Then nothing.

Surfacing to consciousness, he focused on the most vibrant set of blue eyes he'd ever seen. Vibrant and tinged with sadness.

"What…?"

"Stay quiet and follow my lead." Destiny kissed him, a warm, needy kiss that brought his body back to life.

She straightened and looked over him. "He was wounded in a battle with his brother," she said.

"Yet he managed to bring you to us?"

"Yes."

"Yes, *masters.*"

"You are not my masters," she said.

Kade turned his head. Satan's tears, he was lying at the foot of the Grigori council steps. The dark leaders were lined up above him in a judgmental pose. What had she done?

"In time, you will come to call us all 'master,'" the Chief Council said, the others nodding in agreement.

And she was dead.

How could Kadenshar defend her against these creatures? How did they get here? He didn't remember traveling through the portal, bringing her to them. He wouldn't have put her in that kind of danger.

He loved her.

She glanced down at Kade. A tender, sad smile curled the corner of her lips, as if she'd heard his thoughts.

With a confident lift of her chin, she addressed the council. "I've come willingly with this demon."

"Willingly? Only a mortal would be so foolish."

"I am both mortal and para. I am the Crystal Goddess of the prophecy and I've come to make a proposal."

Out of the corner of his eye Kade saw two guards approach. Savage saints, he could do nothing to help her!

"We don't listen to empty mortal lies," the Chief Council said. The guards closed in, but she extended her arms, holding a stone in each palm. The guards halted as if their boots were stuck in cement.

When had she become so powerful?

"As the Crystal Goddess, the purpose of my existence is to keep balance, much like your purpose here in the dark realm. I am no threat and I mean you no harm."

"You think we fear you?" the Chief Council boomed.

"I would not insult you by saying such a thing. However, know that if I am destroyed or tortured, your portals to the mortal realm will close forever. There will be no bridging to familiars, and you will lose access to the world you are meant to visit. This is not a threat, great leaders of the dark realm. This is reality."

The Chief Council motioned for his guards to step back. They did and Destiny lowered her arms.

"You are not in danger of anything I might do, but there is a disease running through your demons that could prove devastating to the dark realm."

"What disease?"

"A mind disease. It craves power and destruction. It is irrational in nature. Kadenshar's brother has it. The demon named Pagroe has it. They are being held in crystals at Cadre headquarters. I will study this illness and work to cure it before it causes more damage to your kind."

"Why would you want to help us, mortal?"

"That is what I do. I heal using crystal magic."

Another council member stepped forward. "But if you are the goddess of the prophecy, isn't your power tied to an Ash Demon?"

She glanced at Kade. "Not if he betrays me. This Ash Demon betrayed me and ruined any chance of a partnership. I need no Ash Demon to fulfill my destiny."

Kade's mortal heart ached at the pain in her eyes. It was over. She could never love him after what he'd done.

"He is a loyal and true soldier of the Grigori," she said. "His only thought was to free demons and return them to your service. He will serve you well as a leader of the Ash race."

No, he didn't want to lead the Ash Demons, didn't want to live without Destiny at his side.

"If my proposal is acceptable to the Grigori, I will take my leave and continue my work."

The Chief Council motioned with his hand as if swatting a pesky insect. "Away, then!"

She bowed to the council, flung her arms above her head and cried out. A flash of golden light blinded him. When he opened his eyes, she was gone.

Destiny.

Gone.

He couldn't breathe, felt as if his mortal lungs had been ripped from his chest.

"You've done well, Kadenshar," the Chief Council said. "You brought us the healer. She may be of use to us."

Kade stood but couldn't speak. He'd lost the woman he loved, his reason for living.

No, he was a warrior. He would not give up that easily.

"She is part mortal. I do not trust her."

"*You* are part mortal," the Chief Council challenged.

"My heart is that of an Ash Demon warrior," he said. "Allow me to fulfill my duty, follow her back to St. Yve Manor and make sure she keeps her word. I will sacrifice myself to keep watch over her for the rest of her days on Earth."

"You would live in the wretched mortal realm indefinitely?"

"To serve the Grigori, yes."

To live with my love, absolutely.

"If you stay in their world, you risk becoming mortal."

"I understand."

He would sacrifice anything for the woman he loved.

"You would risk your demon self for this assignment?"

"I would."

The Chief gathered his council. They discussed, nodded, and then the Chief Council turned back to Kade. "You will report back to us with her progress."

"Yes, master."

"We accept your sacrifice, Ash warrior."

With a wave of the Chief Council's black, gnarly hand, Kade was sucked back into the portal.

But was it too late? Had Destiny hardened her heart to him for all eternity?

No, she loved him. Why else would she have risked her life to bring him back to the Grigori? She knew of their volatility, their uncontrollable fury. There was no guarantee they wouldn't destroy her the moment they laid eyes on her angelic form.

But there *was* a guarantee they would have killed him if he hadn't brought her to the council.

She had risked her life to save his.

She still loved him.

He closed his eyes and traveled through the portal, the bright light at the end calling to him, the light of his love, Destiny, the Crystal Goddess.

Chapter 16

The confrontation with the Grigori had drained Destiny's energy. Once back in the mortal realm, she rushed to the healing pond.

A few minutes longer at the Grigori council and she would have collapsed at their feet. Their dark energy oozed from their beings, sucking the light from her body. And if they'd sensed her weakness, they would have instinctively gone for the kill, no matter what legends and prophecies said about her death closing off demon portals.

She'd stretched the truth about all demon portals being affected by her death when it was only those used by Ash. But she'd been convincing enough to save her life.

And Kade's.

Taking a deep breath, she clutched the polished malachite stone to her stomach as she walked. The stone would help her realign her DNA and cell structure from her trip into the dark realm.

She also pressed the rose quartz to her heart.

But she knew it would never heal.

Her lungs started to tighten and her pulse raced. Had to get into the water, heal her physical condition from having absorbed the Grigori's energy.

No, girl, that's not what's ailing you.

A sob caught in her throat, her emotions bittersweet. Kade would be safe, alive—and masterful as an Ash warrior. He had redeemed himself by bringing her to the Grigori and opening negotiations between them. He would be hailed a hero of the dark realm.

She spotted the healing pond and picked up her pace. She hated where her mind was going, taking her to that dark abyss of sadness. But she'd never felt love before, not that kind of love.

And now she would miss it for the rest of her life.

Placing the malachite in the pouch around her neck, she peeled off her clothes as if they were on fire. She craved the water, needing it to ease the pain of heartbreak.

You let him go because you love him. Appreciate that you loved with a woman's heart.

With a cry of frustration she jumped into the water, seeking peace. The water warmed slightly around her body. She must be fighting a fever.

She broke through the surface and stood. Her eyes closed, arms out, palms up, she bowed before the great power of light energy and calmed her breath. She opened her heart and surrendered.

Hear me, great power. Heal me. I am your messenger of light.

As her heartbeat slowed, she focused on the image of the rose quartz stone that hung around her neck.

The love stone.

"Magic waters, fill my heart, calm my soul." The water grew warmer.

Make me whole, she thought.

But it was never to be.

I am here, my love.

Then she heard a splash.

She felt the red-hot energy of the Ash Demon she loved wading through the water toward her.

She must be dreaming, hallucinating.

Her eyes shot open and she turned to find her lover standing naked beside her.

"What are you doing?" she asked.

"Making you whole."

With a tender smile, he reached out and grazed his fingers along her cheekbone.

"The Grigori," she whispered but closed her eyes against his gentle touch.

"I've been assigned by the Grigori to spend the rest of my days alongside you and make sure you keep your promise."

Her eyes shot open.

"My idea." He smiled.

"But you could change into a—"

"Shhh." He traced his thumb across her lips. "I am dead without you in my heart. Can you forgive me?"

"Forgiving is the first step to healing."

"What's the second?"

She interlaced her hands behind his neck and pulled him close, kissing him with mindless abandon. Kadenshar was here, with her. And just as she'd sacrificed her love to keep him safe, he sacrificed his world to love her.

He broke the kiss and aimed those amazing green eyes at her. "I have other healing skills. Would you like to see them?" He slid his open palm across her breast and down, between her legs.

"You're bad," she breathed.

"I'm demon. And I love you."

* * * * *

Brad shoved the truck into gear and drove to the bottom of the hill, where the road forked. Turn left, and he'd be home in five minutes. Turn right, and he was headed for Indian Rock.

He had no damn business going to Indian Rock.

He had nothing to say to Meg McKettrick, and if he never set eyes on the woman again, it would be two weeks too soon.

He turned right.

He couldn't have said why.

He just drove straight to the Dixie Dog Drive-In.

Back in the day, he and Meg used to meet at the Dixie Dog, by tacit agreement, when either of them had been away. It had been some kind of universe thing, purely intuitive.

Passing familiar landmarks, Brad told himself he ought to turn around. The old days were gone. Things had ended badly between him and Meg anyhow, and she wasn't going to be at the Dixie Dog.

He kept driving.

He rounded a bend, and there was the Dixie Dog. Its big neon sign, a giant hot dog, was all lit up and going through its corny sequence—first it was covered in red squiggles of light, meant to suggest ketchup, and then yellow, for mustard.

Brad pulled into one of the slots next to a speaker, rolled down the truck window and ordered.

A girl roller-skated out with the order about five minutes later.

When she wheeled up to the driver's window, smiling, her eyes went wide with recognition, and she dropped the tray with a clatter.

Silently Brad swore. Damn if he hadn't forgotten he was a famous country singer.

The girl, a skinny thing wearing too much eye makeup, immediately started to cry. "I'm sorry!" she sobbed, squatting to gather up the mess.

"It's okay," Brad answered quietly, leaning to look down at her, catching a glimpse of her plastic name tag. "It's okay, Mandy. No harm done."

"I'll get you another dog and a shake right away, Mr. O'Ballivan!"

"Mandy?"

She stared up at him pitifully, sniffling. Thanks to the copious tears, most of the goop on her eyes had slid south. "Yes?"

"When you go back inside, could you not mention seeing me?"

"But you're Brad O'Ballivan!"

"Yeah," he answered, suppressing a sigh. "I know."

She rolled a little closer. "You wouldn't happen to have a picture you could autograph for me, would you?"

"Not with me," Brad answered.

"You could sign this napkin, though," Mandy said. "It's only got a little chocolate on the corner."

Brad took the paper napkin and her order pen, and scrawled his name. Handed both items back through the window.

She turned and whizzed back toward the side entrance to the Dixie Dog.

Brad waited, marveling that he hadn't considered incidents like this one before he'd decided to come back home. In retrospect, it seemed short-sighted, to say the least, but the truth was, he'd expected to be—Brad O'Ballivan.

Presently Mandy skated back out again, and this time she managed to hold on to the tray.

"I didn't tell a soul!" she whispered. "But Heather and Darlene *both* asked me why my mascara was all smeared." Efficiently she hooked the tray onto the bottom edge of the window.

Brad extended payment, but Mandy shook her head.

"The boss said it's on the house, since I dumped your first order on the ground."

He smiled. "Okay, then. Thanks."

Mandy retreated, and Brad was just reaching for the food when a bright red Blazer whipped into the space beside his. The driver's door sprang open, crashing into the metal speaker, and somebody got out in a hurry.

Something quickened inside Brad.

And in the next moment Meg McKettrick was standing practically on his running board, her blue eyes blazing.

Brad grinned. "I guess you're not over me after all," he said.

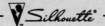

SPECIAL EDITION™

brings you a heartwarming
new McKettrick's story from

NEW YORK TIMES BESTSELLING AUTHOR

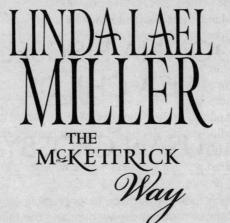

LINDA LAEL MILLER

THE McKETTRICK *Way*

Meg McKettrick is surprised to be reunited with her high school flame, Brad O'Ballivan, who has returned home to his family's neighboring ranch. After seeing Meg again, Brad realizes he still loves her. But the pride of both manage to interfere with love...until an unexpected matchmaker gets involved.

—— McKettrick Women ——

Available December wherever you buy books.

Get ready to meet

THREE WISE WOMEN

with stories by

DONNA BIRDSELL, LISA CHILDS

and

SUSAN CROSBY.

Don't miss these three unforgettable stories
about modern-day women and the love
and new lives they find on Christmas.

Look for *Three Wise Women*
Available December wherever you buy books.

HARLEQUIN®

The Next Novel.com

HN88147

REQUEST YOUR FREE BOOKS!

2 FREE NOVELS PLUS 2 FREE GIFTS!

Silhouette®

n o c t u r n e ™

Dramatic and Sensual Tales of Paranormal Romance.

YES! Please send me 2 FREE Silhouette® Nocturne™ novels and my 2 FREE gifts. After receiving them, if I don't wish to receive any more books, I can return the shipping statement marked "cancel." If I don't cancel, I will receive 4 brand-new novels every other month and be billed just $4.47 per book in the U.S. or $4.99 per book in Canada, plus 25¢ shipping and handling per book plus applicable taxes, if any*. That's a savings of about 15% off the cover price! I understand that accepting the 2 free books and gifts places me under no obligation to buy anything. I can always return a shipment and cancel at any time. Even if I never buy another book from Silhouette, the two free books and gifts are mine to keep forever.

238 SDN ELS4 338 SDN ELXG

Name _____ (PLEASE PRINT)

Address _____ Apt. #

City _____ State/Prov. _____ Zip/Postal Code

Signature (if under 18, a parent or guardian must sign)

Mail to the Silhouette Reader Service™:
IN U.S.A.: P.O. Box 1867, Buffalo, NY 14240-1867
IN CANADA: P.O. Box 609, Fort Erie, Ontario L2A 5X3

Not valid to current Silhouette Nocturne subscribers.

Want to try two free books from another line?
Call 1-800-873-8635 or visit www.morefreebooks.com.

* Terms and prices subject to change without notice. NY residents add applicable sales tax. Canadian residents will be charged applicable provincial taxes and GST. This offer is limited to one order per household. All orders subject to approval. Credit or debit balances in a customer's account(s) may be offset by any other outstanding balance owed by or to the customer. Please allow 4 to 6 weeks for delivery.

Your Privacy: Silhouette is committed to protecting your privacy. Our Privacy Policy is available online at www.eHarlequin.com or upon request from the Reader Service. From time to time we make our lists of customers available to reputable firms who may have a product or service of interest to you. If you would prefer we not share your name and address, please check here. ☐

SN07

NEW YORK TIMES
BESTSELLING AUTHOR

DIANA PALMER

has done it again—created
a Long Tall Texans
readers will fall in love with...

IRON COWBOY

Available March 2008
wherever you buy books.

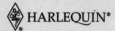

ATHENA FORCE

Heart-pounding romance and thrilling adventure.

She's their ace in the hole.

Posing as a glamorous high roller, Bethany James, a professional gambler and sometimes government agent, uncovers a mob boss's deadly secrets…and the ugly sins from his past. But when a daredevil with a tantalizing drawl calls her bluff, the stakes—and her heart rate—become much, much higher. Beth can't help but wonder: Have the cards been finally stacked against her?

ATHENA FORCE

Will the women of Athena unravel Arachne's powerful web of blackmail and death…or succumb to their enemies' deadly secrets?

Look for

STACKED DECK

by *Terry Watkins.*

Silhouette®

nocturne™

COMING NEXT MONTH

#29 HOLIDAY WITH A VAMPIRE • Maureen Child and Caridad Piñeiro

Celebrate this winter with two chilling tales. In "Christmas Cravings," Grayson Stone returns home to find someone else sleeping in his bed. What in the woods is so terrifying that it has Tessa Franklin running into the arms of a vampire?

In "Fate Calls," death and destruction have been the only gifts Hadrian has received in nearly two thousand years—until the advent of Christmas delivers Connie Morales. Strong enough to escape his thrall, does she have what it takes to heat the blood of a man who claims to have no soul?

#30 THE EMPATH • Bonnie Vanak

Once the leader of a dwindling pack of Draicon, werewolf Nicolas Keenan is now ostracized, and needs the help of Maggie Sinclair. To save his pack, Nicolas draws upon their instantaneous attraction to convince this gentle-natured healer that she is not only his pack's missing empath—and the one person who can fight the forces of darkness—but that Maggie is also his destined mate....

SNCNM1107